Bran's Secret

"Stop. Stop. Oh, please, Dad, stop!"

Bran's excited voice startled Josh Murray. He stamped on the brakes.

"What in the world...?" Josh's voice was impatient. He had been up half the night with a calving cow, and was longing to have a quick nap before evening surgery.

"The house! That house! Just look at it!"

Bran was out of his seat, through the door and on to the road, and was dancing with impatience.

"Can't you see? There through the trees. It's our dream house. Our dream come true. And it's for sale."

Also available in Lions

The House of Secrets

1

Bran's Secret

Joyce Stranger

Lions
An Imprint of HarperCollinsPublishers

First published in Great Britain in Lions in 1994
Lions is an imprint of the Children's Division,
part of HarperCollins Publishers Ltd
77-85 Fulham Palace Road
Hammersmith, London W6 8JB
3 5 7 9 10 8 6 4 2

ISBN 0 00 674831 7

Printed and bound in Great Britain by
HarperCollins Manufacturing, Ltd, Glasgow

Bran's Secret

CHAPTER 1

Bran had spent one of the most exciting days he could remember in all his twelve years. He had his father to himself, a luxury so rare that he could not remember the last time it had happened. The other three had always been there, clamouring for attention.

He was always the last one, even though he wasn't the youngest. This time he was the last to get chicken pox. Now the itching was over, he began to feel energetic again, but a cold which started the day he was due back to school had given him a few feverish days.

A week to recover, his doctor mother had decreed; so here he was, being allowed to visit the farms with his father, and revelling in being the only one of the Murray children on the scene. He wanted to be a vet too, and longed to go out with his father on all his calls, learning as much as he could.

They had begun the day by visiting an out-of-the-way farm to see a Jersey cow with milk fever. Bran loved the toffee-coloured cattle with their huge dark eyes and enquiring noses. Milking had just ended and the patient little brown dog was herding them out to the big field just beyond the barns.

There was so much to see. Fat white geese honked at him as he passed the muddy-edged pond where ducks dived for food. A brown mare stood, watching him, her foal sheltered behind her, almost out of sight. He could see the thin legs and the half-formed tail, and watched in amazement as the little creature collapsed on to the ground. Its mother nosed it, encouraging it to stand again.

It must have been born that morning.

The dog came back to sniff Bran, smelling cats, and then wagged his tail briefly and trotted off to lie in the shelter of the straw in the open barn. The curly-haired farmer gave Bran a quick smile, then closed the field gate and walked over to him.

A tabby cat, with a half-grown kitten beside her, was lapping at a bowl of milk. If only I could live on a farm, Bran thought, as he looked into the nearest sty, finding himself nose to nose with a large black and white pig. He had huge ears and mean yellow eyes; his cheeks and ears were black. A large white streak circled the pig's mouth and reached all the way up to his forehead.

"That's a Berkshire," the man said. "Used to be sandy, and much bigger long ago, when Victoria was Queen. Breeding changed them. That's our top boar, Genghis Khan. I wouldn't want to meet him on one of his bad days."

He scratched the pig's nose and Genghis grunted, standing with his front paws on the half door.

"Come in and have a bite to eat. I'm for breakfast. Your dad'll be in in a bit, when he's seen to Rosie."

The farmer's wife was small and dark, with big brown eyes and closely-curled black hair.

"Come and get warm," she said. A fire blazed in the grate. The huge table was covered with a scarlet cloth. She handed her husband the biggest plate of food Bran had ever seen. It was piled high with bacon, three eggs, fried bread, tomatoes and five sausages, not to mention fried potatoes.

"Put that inside you," she said, laughing at Bran, who couldn't hide his surprised expression. "Tony's been working since five this morning. Needs a lot of energy to do the work here. He's a big man. Would make two of your dad."

"Dawn till dark, and before dawn in winter," Tony said, eating as if he hadn't eaten for weeks.

Bran sat in the big kitchen, regaled with scones, jam and cream, and creamy milk from the Jersey cows. Shire horses paraded on the wallpaper, and a calendar on the wall had a picture of two more shires ploughing. There were model cows on the dresser, jugs shaped like cows, and on the windowsill were two china Shires pulling a brewery cart, its tiny beer barrels stacked high.

A pretty grey cat lay in a box by the fire, her four kittens covered in soft plush fur. One of the kittens tumbled out of the box and staggered across the mat. Bran picked it up, just as his father and the farmer came into the room.

"Look, Dad." Bran's voice was pleading. He could never resist a baby animal.

"Six cats is quite enough," Josh said, though, like Bran, he was entranced by the small playful creatures that swarmed up his legs and cuddled trustingly under his chin, all purring in unison.

Bran didn't want to go, but a vet couldn't spend hours on one farm visit. There was one more call to make. They were to have their lunch on the way. Grandma Bridie had packed sandwiches and fruit and cake, plus a big flask of coffee.

Josh hoped they could get back home in time for him to have a rest before his waiting room filled up again for the evening clinic. They were both eager to get home, but a phone call asking them to go on another visit came through on Josh's mobile phone while they were eating their breakfast.

The extra visit was to a new client. Bran looked at the map; if they took one of the back lanes they could cut some time off the journey, he thought. Bran was bored and was still thinking about his fabulous day when he noticed the sign.

"Stop. Stop. Oh Stop! Please, Dad, stop!"

Bran's excited voice startled Josh Murray. Bran was always so quiet and self-contained. This was exceptional. His father stamped on the brakes.

"What in the world?" Josh's voice was impatient. He had been up half the night with a calving cow, and was longing to have a quick nap before evening surgery.

"The house! That house! Just look at it!"

Bran was out of his seat, through the door and on to the road, and was dancing with impatience. His excitement had taken him over completely. He even forgot how difficult he always found it, telling other people his feelings.

"Can't you see? There through the trees. It's our dream house, our dream come true. And it's for sale."

Josh's eyes followed his son's pointing finger. The estate agent's notice board leaned into the dense and overgrown hedge. He climbed out of the car, and walked to the drunken fence, each paling leaning at a crazier angle than the next. He peered through the overgrown, shrubby bushes that choked the long-neglected garden.

"It's been empty for some time," he said.

It was mid-September and the early autumn sunlight shone on the house's soft red bricks. The roof, badly in need of re-thatching, covered a sprawling building that seemed to have endless rooms. Its tiny leaded windows were thick with grime.

Bran grabbed his father's hand and pulled at

him in a determined effort to get him through the gate, which sagged on its hinges and creaked noisily when Josh thrust it open. Beyond the house, on the far side, a stable door hung open, revealing its dusty interior. An enormous iron-framed enclosure, overgrown with weeds, contained a large dog kennel.

Bran was dancing around the grounds, totally beside himself. He had never wanted anything so much in his life.

"It's perfect, Dad," he said. "We can have a dog; a dozen dogs. And the cats can wander freely. There's no danger from a busy main road, and look at those fields where they can explore!"

He raced round the corner of the house.

"Dad!"

His yell brought Josh running.

"Look. The barn. It could be turned into a surgery and waiting room and offices, and an operating room; it's enormous and it's in pretty good condition. We can have a *proper* house, a *real* house, with rooms we can use downstairs and no need for people to bring their animals in at all."

"It would be wonderful," Josh Murray said. "Just think. Nobody to complain when the dogs in the hospital bark. No noise from the street. A garden instead of a yard, and room to make a proper car park instead of people having to park in the street, or having to walk a long way with their dogs because there isn't a parking space."

He was walking round the house as he spoke.

"It all depends on the price. Come on, let's look round the gardens. There must be a couple of acres here. Room for all kinds of things, if only we could get planning permission."

A huge greenhouse with lots of broken panes had been built against a high brick wall.

The sun gilded the trees that huddled round the house, glinted from the silvery leaves of shining ornamental poplars, then splashed across a line of hollies that promised Christmas berries. It was reflected from the mirror-like surface of the lake, just beyond the low wall that separated the back garden from the fields and woods. A line of rowan trees at the edge of the garden was bright with berries. Two swans floated serenely, a file of grey cygnets trailing behind them.

Beyond them ducks dabbled, their tails in the air, making Bran grin. There was nothing sillier than a duck feeding under the water, its busy tail feathers waggling, he thought.

"It's too good to be true," he said, sadly,

reality overwhelming him.

They stood and looked. It was their dream house, the house they talked about each time the neighbours opposite held one of their endless parties and car doors slammed until early morning.

The house they talked about when none of them could sleep for the incessant cacophony of drums as the group down the road practised for one of their gigs. The four boys dreamed of being famous. Their constant practising and the throbbing beat drove everyone crazy.

The perfect house that Grandma Bridie was always talking about, sure that, one day, they would find it.

"You never find what you're looking for when you want it," she always said. "You only find it when you aren't thinking about it. Like losing the scissors and finding them when you are looking for the thimble." Grandma was a great one for losing things, especially her glasses.

She told them stories of the house she had lived in as a little girl, and the house that she was sure was waiting just for them. She often spoke about it, dreamt about it and sometimes even drew it. A wonderful house with warm red brick walls and roses growing everywhere.

A house with space and with outbuildings so that the whole of the downstairs didn't have to be turned into the office, surgery and waiting room.

They would buy it, move into it and live happily ever after, uninterrupted by noisy humans, with only the wind in the trees to wake them on stormy nights, and only the sound of birds and bees and animals out in the dark, all living their quiet lives.

This was the house she had drawn, right down to the tiniest detail.

"It is our dream house, isn't it, Dad?" Bran was already making plans. He would have the room with the quaint window under the eaves at the far end of the house, just beyond the front door. It jutted out, so there must be a bay window with a window seat. The peaked roof that covered it gave it an air of mystery, a room somehow apart from the others.

They would restore the garden, grow fruit and vegetables and live like kings. They could have dogs. Bran wanted a dog of his own more than he longed for anything else in his life, but the town house's garden was too small and they had always had to make do with cats.

There was a paddock beyond the garden, which you could reach through a gate. It was overgrown, a mass of nettles, thistles and dock, but that could soon be remedied. Georgie could have a horse. Bran's twin sister lived for her riding lessons.

There was a small isolated summerhouse not far from the lake. A special place which they could make their own; a place where they could play games, and use for hiding secrets. There were all sorts of possibilities.

Bran loved the place. He desperately wanted to own it, to be part of it, to know it was theirs. The woods, the lake, the garden, he would explore them all. He looked up at his father, all his longing showing in his eyes.

"It is our dream house," Josh Murray agreed, thinking of peaceful afternoons spent sleeping to make up for lost nights. And no neighbours to wake him.

He was just as enchanted as his son. They had spoken for years about their "one day house", the home they would have far away from the noise and bustle of the town. There would be space for a hospital and kennels for the invalids.

Grandma Bridie would be able to grow peppers and melons and tomatoes and maybe even orchids in the greenhouse.

Maybe she'd become famous for her orchids.

She had once said she would love to grow those exotic flowers.

Grandma Bridie had come to live with them when Granfer died. She still had so much energy that their town house bored her. She spent so long scrubbing and polishing the house that Josh once jokingly said that everything must be worn through with the amount of elbow grease she used on it.

Josh had fallen in love at first sight, just as Bran had. It was a wonderful house, with so many possibilities. It didn't matter to them that it needed a great deal of work. They could sell their town house for a fortune, buy this for far less, restore a few rooms to live in and work on the rest of the house at their leisure.

Josh had already bought it in his own imagination. He had built a huge hospital complex behind it, well away from the house, to keep dogs that needed intensive care. There would be no one to complain about noise or cars parking or dogs barking. In any case, dogs only barked when there were noises to startle them, and there would be no town disturbances here.

It was only a stone's throw from the water and he would be able to take his fishing rod and snatch a brief hour's fishing. Maybe he'd catch nothing, but he would feel the solitude easing away the weariness that he so often felt after long hours spent with a sick animal needing an operation.

He made a note of the name and telephone number on the board.

"Let's go and find out if we can afford it," he said.

CHAPTER 2

"You can afford it. It's waiting for you," a voice said from the other side of the hedge.

They looked in astonishment at the young woman who appeared suddenly, walking towards them. A slim woman, with long dark hair that shone blue black in the sun. A woman with laughing dark-brown eyes. She wore a skirt made of tiny pieces of patchwork, and an intricately-embroidered blouse, picturing flowers and animals. Over that she had thrown a man's tweed jacket, its elbows patched with leather, that came almost to her knees. Her long slim feet were bare.

She laughed at Josh's astounded expression.

Bran thought he had never seen anyone as strange or as beautiful before.

"Do you live here?" Josh didn't think she suited the house, which looked as if it had empty for some time anyway. "Or are you a nymph from the woods, and we're all just dreaming?"

"No, I am Romana. My parents died when I was small and I lived with my grandmother until she died. She was a Romany, a gypsy woman. I have a caravan over in the woods. I used to travel, but I save wild animals that have been injured and it is not very good for them to keep on moving around. They need quiet and security."

She smiled at them. Bran had never seen such an attractive face.

"Then what are you doing here?"

"I know Mr Bradwell, the agent for the house. He let me buy a plot in the woods from the owners, and I have lived there for some years now. Mr Bradwell asked me to keep an eye on the house, to make sure it doesn't get vandalised. Several people have been to look at it, but they don't want the outhouses, and it's too big for most families. In return for watching over it, I can pick the fruit from the garden."

She held up a basket of ripe blackberries:

they were big, luscious and mouth-watering.

"They're called Himalayan Giants. There are several bushes in the walled garden. Come and see the garden and the back of the house. I'll show you through the windows."

She led the way as if she knew they would follow her. Bran raced up the cobbled path. Moss grew in the cracks between the stones.

He looked at the studded oak front door, and the plaque on the pillar beside it.

"Dad, Dad!" Another yell to startle his father. Romana turned to look at him, smiling.

"He's seen the name of the house."

Josh walked over and read the faded gold lettering.

"House of Secrets. Well, well. What secrets does it have?" he asked.

"Each family makes its own. It's a lucky house and everyone who has lived here achieves their wishes, although not always in the way they expect. It was a farmhouse once, many years ago. Now the land is rented to the farmer next door, so he can have more sheep."

Bran was looking at Romana, who had an odd bulge under her jacket. She saw him looking, and turned back the jacket to show him a hare lying against her, cuddled in a sling.

"He was run over. His back legs were paralysed. I have to keep him warm, so it's easier to carry him around with me," she said.

Josh took the little animal from her. It's small body was twisted, the front legs struggling to move and the hind legs almost motionless.

"He's very tame," he said.

He pushed against the hind paws, and very slightly, they pushed back.

"He's beginning to respond." Josh pressed once more, his hand pushing the back paws, and again he felt a small tremor as the little hare tried to thrust against his hands.

Romana nodded and took the hare from him. She slipped a narrow scarf under his body and held him upright. The front legs moved powerfully, the back legs dragged, and then, quite suddenly the little animal began to twitch them, so that they almost walked.

"He's much better than he was," she said. "I found him ten days ago. He was completely helpless. My grandmother taught me how to make healing drinks from herbs, and I feed him those."

She lifted the hare and put him back in the sling, smiling as he cuddled against her.

"The last people to live here were a young couple. They had longed for a baby for so many years, and no child came. The House of Secrets brought them their child, but they couldn't stay here as the husband worked for a firm that moved to Brussels. Their little girl must be nearly five years old now."

"Why has the house been empty for so long?"

"It has been waiting for the right people," Romana said. "Not everyone wishes to live in such a lonely place. It's a big house, needing a family. There are six bedrooms. The Grants had intended to have a big family; they still do, but sadly not in the House of Secrets."

Bran ran up to the house and stood looking through the windows. The bare rooms were large, bigger than any room in their present house and there were so many of them. A bedroom for each of them. He wouldn't have to share with Liam, who woke too early and talked in his sleep. And Georgie and Jenna could have a room each. A study for his father, a little room for his mother, where she could keep her office records, and even *then* there would be three more rooms downstairs.

"It's meant for you," Romana said. "Did you find it by chance?"

"I've never driven along this road before. I wondered where it went, and from the map it looked like a short cut to my next call," Josh said.

He glanced at his watch. "I'll be late."

"Take the blackberries. A present from the house; to claim you as its next family. I can pick more any time. The garden's overrun with them. I make jam and sell it. I'll make some for you."

"I haven't decided," Josh said. "It needs so much work."

"You'll be back," Romana said. "Bring the basket when you come. I'll hear your engine and I'll be waiting for you. If you don't wish me to visit when you've bought it, then tell me. I don't want to intrude."

"We'd love you to come," Bran said.

His father looked at him.

"You can't buy a house just like that, son," he said, his voice amused. "We have to look inside it, find out the price. It may be damp, or have wet rot or dry rot or just need too much work doing to restore it. We may not be able to afford it. And we have to sell our own house. We'll have to ask your mother. She might hate the place."

"It's a lucky house," Romana said. "It has hidden secrets for each of you. You have two sisters and a brother, yes?"

"How did you know?"

Romana laughed.

"I use my eyes. There's a school cap in the car that belongs to a younger boy. I think he'll be in trouble for forgetting his school cap today."

"Liam's seven," Bran said. "I'm twelve. So's my sister, Georgie."

"Who likes ponies. There's a book on ponies on the back seat and it is nearly always girls who like ponies. And you have another sister."

" How did you know about Jenna? She's grown-up. She's fifteen."

"Very grown-up." Romana sounded as if she were laughing but her face showed no signs of amusement. Then she smiled at Bran. "I've cheated a little bit because I *do* know who you are. I've seen Jenna with her dog at a local dog show. Someone told me she's the vet's eldest daughter. The dog's very handsome."

Bran stared at his father. Jenna didn't have a dog, so how could Romana have seen her?

"Her dog?" Josh Murray said blankly.

"The Harlequin Great Dane. She handles him beautifully. She won the Junior Handlers class with him. Surely you knew?"

"Oh yes," Josh Murray said, but Bran knew

that Jenna had hidden this from all of them and wondered why. Which of his father's clients had Great Danes?

And then he remembered. The Silkroy kennels and David Silk, who was only a year older than Jenna *and* went to the same school. Was that why she had kept her win a secret? She hated being teased and they would have teased her if they thought she had a boyfriend.

"I've seen her training him in the big paddock at the stables," Romana said.

"You seem to see a great deal, young lady." Josh looked at her and she smiled back at him.

"I have all the time in the world and it's mine to waste or use. I don't want a regular job in case I have sick animals to care for. When I am free I help at one or other of the stables, especially the big one where Tom Greenock trains racehorses. I've seen you there. You may have thought I was a boy. Everyone does."

She twisted her hair away from her face into a knot and grinned up at him. She was suddenly transformed. Bran stared at her: she looked so different.

"It's a mistake everyone makes when I put my hair up out of the way. I have to, as Tom's big stallion thinks it's funny to try and eat it, and that hurts."

27

"Tom calls you Elf." Josh remembered her now. He had also seen her at the stables where Georgie went to ride.

She let her hair fall back over her shoulders.

"He says I look like an elf: brown-faced, dark-eyed and mischievous."

They were walking back down the garden path. Bran stopped to look at the little plaque with the faint gold lettering. The House of Secrets.

If only they could keep it a secret and not let the family know. If only they could buy it as a surprise and suddenly move everyone there, astounding them. Just an arrangement between him and his father, with nobody else involved. Not even his mother, nor Grandma Bridie.

"We must go," Josh said, "or my new client will think I've forgotten her. Her bitch whelped this morning and she wants me to check her and her pups."

He glanced at his watch. There would be no time for a sleep before the evening surgery. They would have to eat on the way. They had wasted far too much time. Romana put the basket of blackberries on the floor behind the driver's seat.

Bran looked back as they drove away and waved. Romana lifted her hand, smiling.

Behind her stood the House of Secrets, its walls golden in the late afternoon sunshine.

Looking at it, Bran knew that Romana was right. Whatever else happened, they would be back.

CHAPTER 3

Bran longed to get home. He had to sit in the car while his father went in to see the bitch and her puppies, as she might have been upset if too many extra people were around. Eventually the owner of the bitch brought him a bar of chocolate and apologised for keeping his father.

At last they turned the corner into their own road.

"Can I tell them? Please?" he asked.

His father did not answer. He was too busy muttering because there was no place to park near their home. The gateway to their private yard was blocked by a large estate car. He parked four houses up, and Bran raced back, noticing a car inside the yard which meant that there was probably an emergency.

"It's only an hour till surgery," Josh Murray said, arriving almost at a run. "I wonder who's blocked our gateway this time. See if you can find the owner of that car and ask them to move it, or we'll have trouble. People often come early, and they won't want to park miles away and have to walk down the street."

He hated having to park his car far away from his home. He was carrying his bag of equipment, and everything else that was portable. He was irritated and tired.

"You could have helped me," he said to Bran. "You know as well as I do we can't leave anything in the car unless it's right outside the door."

Bran had been too excited to remember. He felt his father was being unfair. Josh opened the door that led into the waiting room and looked at the little gathering that waited for him.

"Dad, thank goodness you're here," Jenna said. Bran envied her and wished he, too, were fifteen and almost grown-up. "I've got everything ready, and Meg's on her way. I rang her up, as I knew you'd want her. This dog's been run over. I knew you'd have to operate."

She didn't need to say why.

The elderly couple who looked up at Josh had a small dog wrapped up in a bloodstained blanket. The dog's eyes stared at him, pleading.

"Children opened the gate. He ran out after them and a car hit him," the woman said. "He's never been out alone before. He was only out for a few seconds."

Josh lifted the little dog into his arms.

"I'll do all I can," he promised, hoping that this time the dog would survive. He hoped that the injuries weren't too severe and that there was not too much pain ahead for the distraught owners.

Bran, not able to tell anybody his news, went through into the kitchen. Meg had just come in at the back door. She was his father's head nurse, a brisk no-nonsense woman with a stocky figure and greying hair, who had time for all the world. The dogs and cats all loved her as much as they loved their owners.

"Bad accident?" she asked Bran.

He nodded, hating the thought of the dog's pain. He knew, from past experience, that it might not survive and he wished Georgie would come home. His twin was closer to him than the other two and at least he could tell her about the House of Secrets and the stable where she would be able to keep a pony.

Liam, who was only seven, was impossible at times. He never stopped chattering, and was always inventing silly rhymes. Sometimes he would suddenly rush off and be an aeroplane or a galloping horse. He had no more concentration than a ten-week-old puppy, Bran thought crossly.

Jenna was too grown up for any of them. She seemed to have her own life and her own world and sometimes didn't appear to belong to the family at all. Except that she could always be relied on in a crisis.

Grandma Bridie came in from the garden, where she had been feeding the cats. She was Bran's mother's mother, a more comfortable version of her daughter.

"Why the long face?" she asked.

"A dog's been run over. Dad's operating," Bran said.

"And the owners?"

"They're there, waiting. Some children let it on to the road."

"Tea and sympathy, "Grandma Bridie said, and vanished through the door. No time to talk to her now either, Bran thought forlornly.

The kettle was always on the Aga and

Grandma would deal with that, but Bran felt it might make him feel better if he helped her.

He put tea in the pot, milk in the jug, found a plate for cakes and scones, put the butter in the dish and laid the table.

"Good boy," Grandma said, as she came through the door with the two silent people. They were as old as she was, Bran thought, and he found himself without words.

"Josh will save him if anyone can." They both sat down, saying nothing, just staring at her. She handed round the scones, which neither the man nor the woman wanted. "I couldn't bear to lose him," the woman said.

"The car didn't stop," the man said.

"Did you see what kind of car it was? You'll have to tell the police."

"A saloon car. Green." The man sipped his tea. "I didn't see the number. I was too worried about Sam." He was neatly dressed, wearing a light suit and waistcoat. His shoes were highly polished, his untidy grey hair gave him an oddly raffish look, as if he had the wrong head on the wrong body. He had been passing his hands through it and it stood on end. As if suddenly aware of this, he tried to smooth it down.

Liam came in and flung his schoolbag down. He grabbed a couple of scones and buttered them, but sensed the atmosphere and looked at Bran. Like Bran, Liam never knew what to say to people he hadn't met before. He chattered endlessly to those he did know well.

He could sense the desperate worry. Bran was suddenly glad that Georgie had a riding lesson. At least *she* wouldn't burst in full of laughter and chatter and upset everyone. Georgie never seemed to realise that other people had feelings. Bran sometimes wondered if she had any at all. She rarely showed them. His sister was so unlike him, even though they were twins, but that didn't stop them being great friends most of the time.

They all looked up as Josh came into the room. Bran thought that his father dwarfed everyone there. He was a big man with wide shoulders and a crown of thick dark hair which only Liam had inherited. Bran and Georgie and Jenna were all blonde, like their mother.

"He's been lucky," Josh said, pouring himself a cup of tea. "A broken leg and a gash on his face. No internal injuries at all. His ear's torn and most of the blood came from that. I've set the leg and plastered it. I'd like to keep him here tonight, to make sure he comes out of the anaesthetic without any problems."

He put a comforting hand on the woman's

shoulder and she looked up at him.

"There's no need to worry. But he's badly shocked. I can keep him warm, as the hospital is well-heated."

"Can we see him?" the woman asked.

Meg came into the room, carrying the little dog. He was a whippet, with short and smooth toffee-coloured fur. He was still sound asleep.

"Come and see him settled, and then you'll know where he is and won't worry so much," Meg said. She smiled at them, her eyes warm and reassuring. "I promise you, in a day or two you're going to have a problem keeping him from rushing around. We've stitched his face, and that won't even leave a scar. He's a very lucky little dog."

The children looked away, embarrassed, as the woman began to cry. Grandma offered tissues, put an arm around the woman's shoulders and led her into the little recovery room behind the kitchen.

A cat that had been spayed that morning mewed to them softly as it was brought in and a Golden Retriever, operated on earlier that day for a small growth on his ear flap, beat a welcome with his tail.

"See, none of them is afraid," Meg said.

She opened the door of one of the bigger

cages, and laid the little dog on the soft blanket inside. A smaller Aga than the one in the kitchen stood in the far corner of the room; towels and dog and cat rugs hung above it to air.

"Waiting room's already filling up," Jenna said, putting her head round the door. "Three cats, a Bulldog, a Boxer and a man outside with a very pregnant goat."

"She's been trying to kid all day," Meg said. "He rang just before I left this afternoon. I told him to bring her and we'd see what needs to be done. I'll put her in the outhouse."

"Don't know what I'd do without Meg." Josh ate three scones rather fast, took a piece of cake from a tin on the dresser and wandered to the window. He looked out at the garden. A small part of it had been wired off and was completely covered in mesh, so that the cats couldn't escape on to the road. They had lost three in quick succession when they first moved here, just before Liam was born.

Bran glanced at the clock. Five minutes to the start of surgery. He watched his father gulp a cup of tea, and then vanish fast through the door again. His parents always seemed to be on the wing. His mother had her own evening surgery at the busy doctors' practice three miles away.

Life had been a lot easier since Grandma Bridie came to live with them. She sold her own house when Granfer died. Bran missed Granfer, especially his jokes and laughter. Granfer had the rare quality of being able to laugh at himself and at his mistakes; he always found something funny in impossible situations that upset everyone else. His approach to life made even awful events seem bearable.

"So what? We're alive," he'd say. Or "Worse troubles at sea. We're warm and we're dry, we have food to eat and the land doesn't go up and down."

Bran gave his grandmother a sudden affectionate smile as she came back into the room, after seeing the whippet's owners to their car.

"What's that for?" she asked suspiciously, wondering if he wanted to borrow something.

"I'm just glad you're here," Bran said. "Mum and Dad never are." He knew that wasn't fair as he said it.

"Well, now, I don't think that's entirely true. You've spent the whole day with your dad. But someone has to make the money to feed and clothe all you lot, and pay all the bills. It doesn't . . ."

"Grow on trees?" said Bran and Liam together, and Grandma Bridie laughed.

"Money, money. Life's not funny, when you haven't any money," Liam sang in a croaking voice that was meant to imitate some pop star, but nobody was quite sure who.

"Oh, dry up," said a voice from the other side of the room and Bran grinned, as the Mynah bird flapped his wings and glared at him. Jed sometimes managed to make remarks that fitted very well into the conversation.

"Money. That's all anyone ever thinks about in this house," Jenna said, on her way through the kitchen to her bedroom. It was an odd house, Bran thought for the hundredth time, He wondered how many of his friends had homes where the downstairs rooms were used for business and the stairs led from the back part of the house up to what was virtually a flat.

The dining room and sitting room were on the first floor. So was the main bathroom, although there was a small one downstairs next to the room where the nurses sat when they had a spare moment.

The bedrooms were on the third floor, and Josh had added a tiny bathroom for convenience. "Just room to swing a very small kitten," Josh had said, when it was finished. It well-deserved the title of the smallest room.

Grandma Bridie closed the window as the

sudden thumping sound of drums deafened them all. Bran glanced out of the window into the garden.

Tabbycat had found a ping pong ball and was tapping it, then chasing it, sending it several yards and pouncing on it. It was his favourite game. He hissed crossly and patted hard at Trish, the black-and-white cat they had found in a box on the waiting-room step two years earlier. It was his ball and she wasn't having it.

Trish was only allowed to play the ping-pong game when Tabbycat tired of it.

Bran sat with his favourite daydream, of living in their "one day house": the house they had been hoping to find for years, but which had never been found. The House of Secrets was one of a long succession of places that might do. They all hated their town home. In his dream, his parents had retired, they had plenty of money and a wonderful house that was like *other* people's houses.

It had to be the House of Secrets. He had never seen anything he liked so much. It had a garden where dogs could run free, and the cats could roam and there were no cars passing the doors all the time and no drums thumping away down the road.

He could't wait any longer to spill the beans. "Grandma," he said.

But Grandma Bridie was busy making their evening meal and he knew, as he looked at her, that she wouldn't hear a word he said. His mother wouldn't be home until after eight o'clock, and Jenna never listened.

He looked desperately at Liam, who sensed his mood and walked out into the garden. Bran followed.

Georgie, swinging her riding hat, came out to join them, a slice of cake and a scone in her hand.

"We found a house today," Bran said. "Dad and I. It's a wonderful house. It's called the House of Secrets. We're going to buy it."

Liam decided it was more fun to sit on the swing and pretend he was flying a helicopter.

Georgie looked at her brother. Bran was always making up stories. Whoever heard of a house called the House of Secrets? You couldn't buy houses quickly anyway. They were stuck with this place. She looked at it, the big ugly building set in the middle of a housing estate which had been built much later, crowding it.

Outside the front gate a car hooted, brakes squealed, and playing children yelled at the tops of their voices.

41

The steady rhythm of the drums banged into Bran's brain. He hated this place and looked up at the sky to make a wish.

"Let us find a real house to live in, quickly, please," he said, hoping God would hear him and make his wish come true. "A house where I can have a dog."

He looked at Georgie, sighing, knowing that she didn't believe the house was real, and went indoors miserably. The whole wonderful day was spoiled because no one would listen to him.

Maybe he had slept in the car and dreamt the house, after all. It seemed remote now; unreal, as if it had never existed. He longed for his father to finish surgery and to come and eat with them.

But when surgery was over Josh made himself a couple of sandwiches, wolfed a cup of coffee and vanished with Meg to help the goat have her kid.

Nobody would ever listen to him, Bran thought. He went up to his bedroom, which was right at the top of the house. He shared it with Liam. It was tiny, with a sloping ceiling, and had just enough room for the two bunk beds and a wardrobe. Sometimes Bran felt as if the room was squashing him. He was suddenly tired of all his family.

Georgie came in.

"I wish you had *really* found a house," she said. "It would be wonderful to have somewhere to live away from here."

"It's in the country," Bran said. "It has a lake beyond the garden, and there are swans. Dad said it's perfect."

Georgie was suddenly jealous of Bran, who had had their father to himself for a whole day. She didn't want to pretend to believe him.

"And I suppose there were whales in the lake and peacocks in the garden and a gold mine just outside the front door."

She went out, shutting the door hard, feeling miserable because she had been mean. Downstairs in the kitchen Liam and Grandma Bridie were chattering away together.

"Both kissed the Blarney Stone," their mother often said.

Bran slipped down the stairs, went out of the back door into the garden and sat by his imaginary German Shepherd. He had invented Troy when he met Hero, the big police dog that came to Josh for attention. Hero was an enormous dog with bounding energy and a tail that wagged pleasure whenever he met Bran. If only Bran had a *real* dog beside him to sense his mood. He would lick his neck and then lie with his head on Bran's knee.

You can't be lonely if you have a family, Bran thought, but he knew *he* was.

He went back to his bedroom and was comforted when Tabbycat came in through the door and settled, purring at his feet. The cat knew he would be evicted if anyone else found him, but there was a secret place at the foot of Bran's bed under the eiderdown that only the two of them knew about.

His mother had not come home by bedtime. His father and Meg were still busy with the goat, who had twins. There were major problems. Bran lay and watched the dusty plane trees dancing in the shadows cast by the streetlamp outside his window. The throbbing drums beat on. His family had complained to the council *and* to the police, but nothing made any difference. One or two days of peace; then the noise started again. It was hours before Bran managed to fall asleep and even then the incessant beat sounded in his dreams.

CHAPTER 4

Next day was Friday the 13th. It was going to be a terrible day. Bran knew it as soon as he woke. The sky was grey and it was raining. A delivery lorry groaned past his window, its gears grating as they changed down for the hill. Children were yelling to one another as they raced down the road for the bus.

He waited until the house was quiet before he got up, feeling that he didn't belong in the real world at all. Both his mother and his grandmother treated him as if he were still ill, and he wasn't. He wished he could have gone back to school.

"Monday is time enough," his mother said.

"That was a very nasty cold indeed, and you had chickenpox very badly too."

Everyone was racing around and he was lying there, listening, keeping out of the way of the morning rush for the bathroom.

Liam left a trail of questions behind him, and his busy little feet seemed to patter endlessly past the bedroom door. Bran kept his head under the covers and pretended to be asleep while his small brother dressed. He didn't feel sociable. He felt at odds with everyone, and didn't know why.

Liam's shrill voice echoed up the stairs.

"Where's my PE kit? Someone's pinched my gym shoes. My cap's gone. I can't find it anywhere."

"You left it in the car," Grandma Bridie's voice said. "It's where it ought to be now, on the hall stand."

"Someone's hidden my homework."

Grandma Bridie soothed and consoled. Bran knew she would be finding everything, quietly and competently, and seeing that Liam caught the school bus at the corner of the road.

His father had to test a herd of Friesian cattle on a distant farm, to make sure none of them had brucellosis, which was, as far as Bran could make out, pretty horrible for cows and people.

He must get the big veterinary dictionary and find out more about it. All he knew was that it made cows lose their calves before they were born. Bran wanted to go with him, but Josh said no, he would be too busy and Bran would get bored.

He *wouldn't* be bored. He wanted to watch, to see how his father did the tests and to see how the cows behaved. He wished they lived near a farm, so he could help with the milking and feeding. He'd like to be a farmer but there was no chance of that. No, one day he would be a vet too.

Maldwyn, his father's assistant, was on duty and if there was one thing Maldwyn hated more than he hated Christmas, it was children. It would be better to keep out of the way all day. Bran sighed. Maldwyn rushed past all of them as if they didn't exist and looked horrified if any of them spoke to him.

Bran heard his mother's voice as she stood in the yard, ready to get into her car.

"Expect me when you see me. It's ante-natal day. I can never get them to go home; they have so many questions."

He heard Grandma Bridie reply:

"And you love every minute of it!"

He knew his mother wouldn't have heard,

because she was already revving the engine.

"Don't blame me if you burst the engine," Grandma Bridie's voice said tartly. Only Bran knew it wasn't Grandma. It was Jed. There were times when the Mynah said the oddest things. Someone had brought the bird in a couple of years ago for Bran's father to look after for a few days. The owner had never come back. Jed had silent days, but today was obviously a talking day and that meant he would be very noisy indeed. He was a handsome bird with gleaming feathers, brilliant shining eyes and a spectacular beak that reached out and pecked the unwary.

"Poor Jed's lonely. Talk to Jed," the voice said, this time in Jenna's voice. Sometimes nobody knew who was really speaking. Jed cackled wickedly and then whistled, "Coming through the Rye," out of tune. That was Liam.

Jenna was the next to leave. She moved like a ghost: soft-footed, neat and tidy, gathering everything together quietly, slipping out of the house with a quick kiss on Grandma Bridie's cheek, before fetching her bicycle. Bran heard the shed door close.

His father had already left, taking Meg with him to keep the records. Georgie was late. She came clattering downstairs, shouting to

Grandma Bridie to find her school hat, her blazer, her homework, and gobbling her breakfast toast with half an eye on the clock and getting dressed as she ate. Bran could imagine every movement. Georgie was hopeless, often making all of them late as they waited for her last minute dash around the house.

He made up for her lack of organisation by always being early. This only made him more annoyed when he had to wait for his twin.

"I wonder you have time to breathe," his grandmother said. Her voice was irritated.

He could imagine her watching Georgie impatiently, taking the comb and thrusting it through her granddaughter's mane of thick fair hair, pulling it back into the ribbon that bound her ponytail, Georgie complaining bitterly. Georgie never remembered to brush her hair when she got up.

"You're hurting," Georgie said.

Jed mimicked. "Hurting, hurting, hurting."

"I hate that bird. I wish Dad would get rid of him." Georgie was out of the house, the door slamming behind her, and Bran knew that she would be shrugging into her blazer as she ran, thrusting on her hat, dragging her schoolbag. She would catch the bus with only seconds to spare. Bran usually watched her from the bus, agonising every day because he felt sure she would miss it.

He heard Maldwyn greet Grandma Bridie. She would offer him toast and coffee and he would sit and chat to her until surgery began. Cars had already arrived. Maldwyn was going to be busy.

If they lived in the House of Secrets the surgery would be away from the house. There would be room for dozens of cars to park, unlike at their town house where latecomers had to find parking spaces where they could, and had to carry or drag sick animals along the pavement to the waiting room.

When would his father go to the estate agent? When would he ever get time?

Bran decide to have a shower. It would fill in half an hour, by the time he was dressed, and he already felt fed up with the day. He couldn't even think of anything he wanted to do.

He spent twenty minutes deciding what to wear. After several false starts, he decided on jeans and a T-shirt with whales on the front and diving dolphins on the back, which his mother had bought him for Christmas the previous year.

He went downstairs, but was alarmed to find Maldwyn coming back into the kitchen. Maldwyn was much younger than Bran's father. He was a stocky man with a thick thatch of curly red hair, astonishingly vivid blue eyes and a quick temper.

When Bran thought about it, he realised that Maldwyn was only ever angry with *people*, never with *animals*, who trusted him implicitly. All their cats adored him.

Maldwyn seemed oddly tongue-tied whenever Jenna was around. None of the children realised that his brusqueness and rudeness was due to extreme shyness. They all thought he hated them.

Being an only child, Maldwyn was used to being alone and had never spent much time with other children. He had been born on a busy farm and lived most of his life among animals, growing up understanding them far better than he understood people.

His boss's children worried him.

He picked up his half-finished cup of coffee. Grandma Bridie was nowhere to be seen and her little yellow Mini was missing from its usual parking place.

"Bran!" Maldwyn's voice was sharp. "There's a problem. Your grandmother's gone to the market. Meg's out with your father and Helen doesn't come in until eleven, and when

I rang her house there was no answer. I've no one in reception or anyone to answer the phone. I can't do surgery was well."

"Helen's at the dentist." Bran always felt tongue-tied when he spoke to Maldwyn. "I expect I can cope. I take messages for Dad and Mum quite often."

Maldwyn's face almost smiled. Bran wondered if he ever laughed. He put two slices of bread in the toaster and poured coffee from the thermos jug that Grandma Bridie always kept full.

There was a note on his plate.

"Gone shopping. Feed cats. Be good. Back about twelve. Gran."

It didn't look as though there was going to be much spare time after all. There were already several people in the waiting room, including one with a cat in a wire carrier. The handsome black Persian had a look of aristocratic disdain, and bawled miserably once in a while. Jed responded with hoots, whistles, and a loud Siamese miaow.

Bran swallowed the scalding coffee, having seen two more owners through the window. He ate a slice of dry toast as he walked round the kitchen collecting cat bowls. He never did find out where Grandma hid the marmalade and margarine, and she had tidied up before she went out.

He opened three small tins of cat food. Half on each plate. No time to do more than put them on the floor of the enclosure and make certain that the door was shut tight; otherwise one of the cats was sure to end up a casualty on the road.

If only he had a dog of his own to feed. He ached for a dog. His imaginary Troy bounded up to him, a slightly smaller version of Hero, and greeted him ecstatically.

The phone was ringing as he raced inside. There were a few more people in the waiting room now, including one with a whining little girl who spent all her time complaining.

"Can we go home now? That dog's going to bite me. I don't like that dog. Why's that cat so noisy?"

Everyone sat silently, pretending they couldn't hear her. Her mother did her best to answer her questions, distract her and keep her quiet, but without any success. The small grizzling voice went on and on. They had a cardboard box with them that probably contained a rabbit, Bran thought.

The phone rang. He made an appointment

for a puppy to have its first protective inoculations that afternoon. Then he remembered that he had to find out each owner's name, the animal's name, *and* find the right cards for Maldwyn.

He also had to take the money and give change, and write down how much each treatment cost. He knew he would make mistakes; it would all be wrong and he'd never be able to manage it.

Everyone seemed to be staring at him and he wished he had chosen a less conspicuous shirt.

"I don't like whales," the child said. She began to chant in a singsong.

Jed, alerted by the noise, added his own contribution.

" Moll's dead. Poor Jed's all alone. Children are noisy. Be quiet, everyone." Bran often wondered who Moll was. Perhaps Jed had once had a mate. The bird added two catcalls, a bark and a whistle, leaving newcomers to the surgery staring in astonishment.

"It's our Mynah bird," Bran said, walking out from behind the counter with a notebook. It would be easier to write down all the names and *then* find the cards, he thought. "He's feeling frisky today."

Maldwyn had already started. A tall woman

with a very small Dachshund came out of the surgery and stood waiting to pay.

"Twelve pounds," Maldwyn said to Bran. "I'll note down all the treatments and drugs. Just jot down the owner's name and the animal's name and the amount paid on a sheet of paper. Helen can write it up when she comes in. Who's next?"

Bran quickly looked at his half-completed list. "Mrs Thomas and Lucky."

"Who's feeling most unlucky," the Persian cat's owner said. "She caught a weasel, but it bit her very badly on the leg before she killed it."

She picked up the cage and followed Maldwyn into the surgery.

Bran moved hastily out of the way as a small man with a very large dog hurtled into the room, the dog barking noisily. Anxious owners drew their animals away and the alarmed man went back through the door faster than he had come in.

"I'll wait outside till surgery ends," he yelled above the din.

Bran was grateful: two other dogs were barking and one very small Jack Russell sat growling steadily, refusing to be quiet. It only needed one noisy animal to disrupt the whole room.

Not being very helpful, Jed barked, and Bran ran into the kitchen, putting the cloth that covered the bird at night over the cage. There was an indignant squawk and then silence.

After two hours Bran was exhausted, confused and very worried. Was the money right? Several people had written cheques, but others had needed change for twenty pound notes. One elderly gentleman had been very impatient indeed, as Bran struggled to take eight pounds and thirty pence from twenty pounds and give him the right money.

The last patient had gone. Maldwyn checked Bran's list against the notes and cheques. The small change added up correctly too.

"You did well," he said. "It isn't easy."

"Jed's all alone," said the Mynah in Bran's voice, as he removed the cover.

"He must have thought he had a very short day," Maldwyn said, suddenly relaxing with Bran. Working together had made them companions. "I wonder what makes him noisier some days than others?"

Jed flapped his wings, and said in Grandma Bridie's voice,

"For heaven's sake, come and have some coffee."

Maldwyn grinned at Bran; a real grin.

"Sounds like a great idea. Let's take the phone into the kitchen, and the appointment book too. It's nearly eleven, and I think we both deserve a break."

He unplugged the phone from the socket behind the desk and re-plugged it in the kitchen. There were sockets in every room, to make sure there was always someone to answer.

Bran poured coffee from the flask into two mugs. "What would your Gran say if we stole two slices of that cake?" Maldwyn asked, looking longingly at the fruit-cake that stood cooling on the windowsill. Grandma was always up before any of them; she said old people didn't need much sleep. She spent the first two hours of every day baking.

Bran remembered that Maldwyn lived in a flat on his own and did all his own cooking. It seemed a bit unlikely that he ever made a cake.

"Be my guest," Jed said, and they both laughed.

"Does he really know what he is saying, or is it all accident?" Maldwyn asked as he cut two large slices of fruit-cake, stiff with sultanas and cherries.

"Accident, accident, accident." Jed flapped his wings and began to preen, throwing out two feathers which fell through the bars of the cage and on to the floor. Tabbycat, who had come indoors with Bran, caught one and raced across the room with his trophy to Grandma's rocking chair, as if afraid someone would steal it from him. He sat tossing it and catching it.

Jed put his head on one side, his eyes glinting at them both. He suddenly produced a yell of maniacal laughter, and then hopped off his roost to the bottom of the cage and looked at them again, his head now tilted to the other side.

"He's one of life's mysteries," Maldwyn said. He laughed suddenly and unexpectedly and looked much younger. "One of my aunts had an African grey parrot when we were children. She inherited it from a sailor who died. It swore abominably but only when she had visitors who would be shocked by its language. I'm sure the wicked bird knew exactly what it was doing. She had to put him in another room when the vicar came to tea."

"Good job Jed doesn't know any real swear words," Bran said. "He's embarrassing enough as he is. The vicar might think we'd taught him. His first owner must have been a very irritable man. Sometimes Jed yells at *everyone* as if he were really furious with them."

They had tried to re-educate the bird, replacing his vocabulary with more suitable words. But there were days when Jed forgot, especially if he were in a bad temper. He was always very grumpy on windy days. The cats became scatterbrained then too and rushed crazily round in circles.

Helen, the receptionist, came through the door and raised her eyebrows. She was slim with a neat dark ponytail which was always tied with a bright ribbon. Bran suspected she had different colours for different days of the week, but he had never worked out the system. Today was blue velvet, embroidered with tiny flowers.

"Having a party? Can anyone join?"

"Coffee and cake?" Maldwyn's face had stiffened again and Bran wished Helen had not come in at that moment. Maldwyn had revealed a different side of himself.

"Go away. Go away. Go away," said Jed with another string of whistles and a long drawn-out miaow.

"How did you cope?" Helen asked thoughtfully. She poured her coffee, and then sat at the table.

"With difficulty, but Bran deserves a medal," Maldwyn said, determined to be generous. "I hope there aren't any emergencies. There are no operations scheduled today as

Josh is away, but it only needs a road accident to change all that."

He glanced at Bran.

"You've got the rest of the day off. Have fun," he said, as he and Helen went back into the waiting room to sort out the morning's entries in the big account book.

Quite suddenly, Bran knew what he wanted to do with the rest of the morning. He would call in at the estate agent's and see if they had the details of the House of Secrets. The office was only in the next street, and nobody would miss him if he popped out.

He zipped up his anorak and glanced back at Jed as he went towards the door.

"You're the only one who ever listens to me," he said. "But it's no use telling you. You couldn't keep a secret if you tried."

"Try, try, try again. Don't succeed," said Jed, with one of his more splendid confusions.

Bran grinned as he shut the door behind him.

CHAPTER 5

The rain hit the dirty pavements and slid down the front of the newsagent's shop at the end of the road. A nagging wind drove discarded sweet wrappers along the street. Houses and shops were shabby with age, everything seemed to need a bright coat of new paint. The worn pavements held puddles that splashed people as they passed. Once a car, driving too close to the kerb, flung up a cloud of spray, which soaked Bran's right side with muddy water.

They were already frying at the chippy and the smell made Bran hungry again. Busy people rushed in all directions as if there was no time to spare.

A reversing lorry blocked the end of the road. Drivers hooted impatiently. Bran slipped between the vehicles, thankful for the holdup. That crossing, according to Helen, was murder. She had to brave it every day on her way from the bus stop. Sometimes Bran thought Helen seemed little older than he was, and much younger than Jenna. She had left school only the previous summer and still had an impish and juvenile sense of humour not always appreciated by her employers.

The estate agent had a large window with an unexpectedly small room behind it. A sulky girl sat at a table in the corner, painting her nails. She glared at Bran as though he were an intruder with no right to be there or to interrupt her.

Bran looked at the pictures of houses and shops; he looked at pictures of the local stables. That would upset Georgie. None of them had realised it was for sale. He could not see a photograph of the House of Secrets.

He had never wanted anything so passionately in his life, because the house would hold the key to all their dreams. The House of Secrets was only four miles from the centre of town so people would still come to his father's surgery. One day it might be Bran's surgery but that was in the unimaginable future, at least twelve long years away.

The girl at the desk was no older than Helen. She wore a very short leather miniskirt, a very tight white jumper, and more make-up than Bran had seen on any face before. Improbably long eyelashes swept her cheeks and Bran just hoped they wouldn't fall off. Huge red plastic hooped earrings dangled almost to her shoulders. Her bright blonde hair was plaited. She held up three painted nails and surveyed them moodily.

"I never get it right. They smudge. I'll have to take it all off."

She wiped away the bright scarlet varnish with cotton wool.

"You wanted something?" Her eyes were on her hands, not on Bran.

"I want the particulars of the House of Secrets," he said. "Please," he added, Grandma Bridie's chiding voice in his mind. "Them as don't ask politely don't get," it reminded him, quoting an old gardener who had been part of her childhood days.

"The what? You must be joking. No house was ever named that."

"This one is."

"Then it must be another agent. I haven't

seen it." She was concentrating on her hands, and scarcely looked at Bran.

"You could look," Bran said, sure that the green filing cabinets must contain details of the houses on sale. He glanced at the headings on the leaflets on the desk. The name of this estate agent was definitely the same as the agent on the board outside the House of Secrets yesterday.

"I wouldn't know where. I'm temping, see? Only came in this morning. Nobody's told me anything yet except to hold the fort and take down the names and addresses of anyone who comes in. You can give me your name and address. What's a little shrimp like you doing wanting particulars? For a school project, I suppose. Wasting our time. You ought to be at school."

Bran was irritated. If anyone was wasting time *she* was. He was sure painting her nails was not part of her daily duties. Besides, he was as tall as she was and certainly didn't feel like a shrimp. He was bigger than half of the boys in his form.

"I want it for my father."

He was suddenly furious, an emotion that surprised him. He rarely lost his temper, unlike Georgie and Liam. They flared up several times each day and yelled at one another and anyone else who happened to annoy them, then forgot what had bothered them and started laughing.

Bran walked across to the first filing cabinet and yanked open the top drawer (A – E). He was just in time to catch it before it slid right out and fell on the floor. He hadn't expected it to move so easily.

Would it be filed under "House" or "Secrets" he wondered; or worse, under the owner's name?

The next drawer was E – J and suddenly there it was, under H as he expected. He slipped the slim folder out.

The House of Secrets.

It was a lucky charm, and the future was hidden in its meagre pages. It was real, it existed and he held the details in his hands. He glanced at the price. He didn't know if it was an enormous sum or not. It looked enormous but then he knew that houses didn't come cheap. Theirs had prime value, his father said. If they sold, it would be knocked down and someone would build a block of flats on the site, with shops on the ground floor.

"Pipe dream," his mother said. "It'll stay on the market for years. Nobody'll want it."

They discussed moving whenever the drums

were at their worst. It was a daydream, something that would never happen.

Reality was in the busy street and the constant noise.

"People won't want to come that far to the vet," his mother said.

"They will if he's good enough."

It was the same old argument that rumbled on in different forms whenever his parents were very tired, which seemed to be more often than ever these days. Bran dreaded Friday nights when Liam was over-tired from the long week and everyone else was short tempered too. It would be different if they moved. There would be peace around the house and the only noises would be birdsong and the calls of the ducks and geese on the lake.

He had been brooding over the house details, and had forgotten where he was.

"You've got a nerve," the girl said. "Coming in off the street and just taking what you fancy." She glanced at the folder. "House of Secrets. What a daft name. It looks horrible. Wouldn't suit me. I like to be in town, not out in the country with nothing to do and mud everywhere and cows and sheep bawling."

Bran couldn't be bothered to tell her that animals only bawled if there was something wrong. Usually they were silent, too busy grazing to make a noise. Sheep only bleated when they were sheared or if the weather turned cold. Or at the gathering, when the dogs were bringing them in to the dip, or if stray dogs and foxes were among the flock. Or when the lambs were taken from their mothers. Cows bawled then too. The children stayed on a farm for their holidays, with Grandma Bridie. Their parents were usually too busy to get away and the family never seemed able to take a holiday at the same time. The farm belonged to one of Grandma's many distant cousins.

The farm was in Devon, near Dartmoor, where the prison stood stark and bleak against the sky. Holidays meant helping on the farm, and scones and jam and cream, and more food than they could eat.

Bran came back to reality.

The girl began to paint the nails on her other hand, totally absorbed. Bran glared at her and walked out of the office, sure she was more stupid than anyone he had ever met. But he had his talisman, his lucky charm. He folded it carefully and slipped it under his anorak to keep it dry. The rain was now beating down heavily, the huge drops hitting the pavement and bouncing back up. The wind blustered, so that people hung on to their hats; Bran wished his anorak had a hood.

He sheltered briefly in a shop doorway but there was no sign that the storm would ease. Thick dark clouds hung low overhead. He ran, but it was several minutes before he crossed the road. There were so few gaps in the traffic. He longed for the quiet lanes around the House of Secrets, and his forehead creased, almost in pain, as he passed the house where the insistent drums were thumping again. He hated the drums and the boys who played them. If only they would move away.

His hand stroked the folder. He couldn't wait to get indoors. He wanted to read it and show it to whoever might be at home.

It was quicker to go in at the waiting-room door. As he opened it a woman came out and she almost collided with him, unable to see because of the tears pouring down her face. Shocked, Bran saw the collar and lead in her hand and realised why she was crying. He moved aside and watched her stumble towards a grey Ford. She fumbled uselessly with her car keys as she tried to open the driver's door.

He glanced around the little yard. No sign of the Land Rover, which meant his father and Meg were still away. Meg would never have let a client come out in a state like that. He ran over to the car, took the keys and opened the door for her.

"I think you ought to come inside with me and sit down for a bit," he said. "Come and talk to my Gran. You can't drive yet." Maldwyn rarely thought about the owners of the animals he put to sleep. It made him too miserable, especially if it were a young dog, dead before its time. He would be upset for the rest of the day. Helen would be in tears, lacking Meg's experience. Meg cried afterwards; when she was alone. He had found her once, her face buried in a cat's fur. She was desolate because one of their long-time patients had had to be helped out of the world because he had cancer. The old Mastiff had been older than Bran himself, a regular visitor and loved by everybody. He had been greeted, petted and fussed over whenever he came there.

The woman put the collar and lead down on the passenger seat. She climbed out of the car and stood facing the house. Bran swiftly picked up the unwelcome reminders and hid them on the floor at the rear of the car. They would not be there to distress her on the way home.

Bran led the woman into the kitchen, where Grandma Bridie was preparing coffee and sandwiches. She took one glance at Bran's companion, put her arm around her and led her to the little sitting room.

Maldwyn came into the kitchen, glanced at Bran and poured hot water on to the instant coffee. He added milk and several spoons of sugar.

"Black Friday. It's bad enough when they're old," he said, his voice angry. "I can't fight that, but I feel cheated every time a young dog dies."

"What happened?" Bran asked.

"A neighbour put down slug pellets in his garden. The dog got through the fence, chasing a cat. Pellets are very poisonous and he must have taken the lot. He hadn't a chance. A gorgeous young Boxer, one of my favourites. Only just over a year old. It's the worst age, as they eat anything at that age."

Bran was always in and out of the waiting room. He listened to the talk at coffee-time whenever he was home. He knew enough to realise that the young dogs were the most likely to die from accident or from eating things that an older dog wouldn't touch. Sometimes older dogs surprised their owners, by suddenly doing something they had never done before, which all too often led to disaster.

Some years ago a local farmer had put down illegal strychnine bait to get rid of foxes. Nobody knew if foxes had taken it, but two dogs and three cats had died.

Helen came into the room, her eyes suspiciously pink.

"I wish people would stop using all these things," she said. "A few weeks ago we had a kitten die from rat poison that had been put under a shed. The owners thought the opening was too small for any pet to get through. This kitten was about nine weeks old. Just the age to experiment with anything he found lying around." She sat, looking desolate. "He was so pretty. A tiny tortoiseshell. He hardly lived at all."

They drank in silence, each busy with their own thoughts. Bran passed around a plate of Cornish pasties. Food was always a consolation. Grandma Bridie came into the kitchen to pour coffee into two of their more elegant cups and to put her special home-made biscuits on a pretty plate. She looked thoughtful.

"You should have called me," she said to Maldwyn, as he looked at her glumly. "No one ought to be left alone to drive home in that state."

Maldwyn opened the door for her, and closed it behind her, saying nothing. Bran thought he looked agitated.

If I ever have a puppy, he thought, I'll be so careful. I couldn't bear it to die like that.

He tried to conjure up Troy, but somehow his imaginary dog couldn't fill his mind with pleasant thoughts.

When Maldwyn and Helen went out of the room, Bran put the details of the House of Secrets on the table in front of him. It looked even more appealing in the brochure, although it was obvious that the outbuildings had been neglected.

It was a colour photograph, taken in the middle of summer. The garden bloomed. It must have been taken when people were still living in the house. The rose that climbed above the porch was in full flower, its golden buds bright against the warm red brickwork. There were photographs of the lake, the fields behind the house, the barn and the kennel enclosure.

Six bedrooms, two bathrooms and a much bigger than the one they had here. A huge kitchen/dining room that Grandma Bridie would love. Large farmhouse-type kitchen, the brochure said. There were two other rooms: a garden room and a sewing room. Who on earth had a sewing room, Bran wondered. He wasn't sure that his mother could sew. Perhaps it would be a little room for Grandma Bridie. She could go there to escape.

Three and a half acres. It hadn't looked that big, but maybe they had not seen all of it. There was the orchard with the paddock alongside. They could convert some of the paddock into a car park. There was enough room for Georgie to have her own pony. He would have his own dog.

Liam . . . he would have room to fly his radio-controlled aeroplane, and the kite that he could only use on rare occasions. There was no room in their town house and they seldom had time to go out and find a place where it was safe. And Jenna? He wondered about Jenna. Maybe she would have a Great Dane puppy. She already *had* a secret. Before yesterday none of them had known she went to dog shows with Dave Silk. "Don't tell the others and don't tell her we know," his father had said, the day before, on the way home. "She'll tell us in her own good time. Maybe there's something she wants to win . . . if she thinks we know it will spoil it for her."

Bran wondered about the other two. Maybe they all had secrets. Maybe everyone had secrets, private things that they did not want anyone else to know. He'd never told anyone about Troy, his wonderful imaginary dog. They'd laugh at him. Did Georgie have a pretend horse? Liam couldn't have any secrets; he couldn't manage to not tell everyone what he'd bought them for Christmas or birthdays. The information just spilled out of him.

Jed was unusually quiet, which Bran thought just as well. He did not want the bird to shout, "Moll's dead. Poor Jed's lonely," in case the Boxer owner heard.

Bran looked down at the photographs of the House of Secrets again. The drums were starting, the beat thundering into his head, drowning even the traffic noise.

"I hate this place," Bran said. "We must move to the House of Secrets."

Jed put his head on one side, listening, and then he repeated the sentence softly. Bran walked out of the room, forgetting about the Mynah bird.

CHAPTER 6

Saturday morning. Bran dressed quickly; he knew his father was not taking the first surgery and his mother had the weekend off. Now he could tell them about the House of Secrets. Maybe they could all drive over and look at it. He knew they'd love it as much as he did. Maybe his father would buy it at once. Bran had no idea how long it took to buy a house. They would have to sell their own. Perhaps they could move before they sold it.

Perhaps Maldwyn would buy their house and they could run two surgeries.

Liam had already finished his breakfast and

gone out to visit a friend by the time Bran came downstairs.

Grandma Bridie put a plate of scrambled egg on toast in front of him.

"Eat. You're beginning to look transparent," she said.

"Where's everybody?"

"Liam's gone fishing with his friend Tony and his father. Georgie's riding. Jenna went off at daybreak on some mysterious adventure of her own. Your mother's gone to the hairdresser."

"Where's Dad?"

"Maldwyn had a problem with his first patient. She's a Burmese cat. She was sitting by a second-floor window which was open. She saw a bird, jumped after it and landed on some barbed wire. She needs an immediate operation and the surgery's fuller than usual. Every dog in the town seems to be in the waiting room. Meg and your dad are operating. She was bleeding badly."

"Miaow," said Jed, as the marmalade cat strolled across the kitchen floor. "Stupid Marmy," he added.

Marmy, who was used to the Mynah, continued towards the door and slipped out through the catflap that led to the cats' enclosure. They had their own little shed, where they slept on warm blankets in a curled together heap. As soon as Tabbycat came in and slipped upstairs to hide under the eiderdown Bran bolted the flap. Not even Liam, who slept in the same room, knew he was there. The cat seemed to know only too well that this was forbidden.

"Dad and I found a house," Bran said, swallowing hastily. "A wonderful house," he added desperately. Grandma Bridie was clattering dishes as she washed up and didn't appear to be listening.

"That's nice," she said. "I think I might make some more Cornish pasties. They go down very well. Everyone seems to have their own things to do today. Goodness knows when they'll all come in for lunch, and they're bound to be hungry, especially Georgie."

Bran wasn't interested in Cornish pasties. Why didn't anyone in the house ever listen to anyone else? He wanted to talk, but Grandma hung up the tea towel, put away the dishes and brought out the big mixing bowl.

"Nobody ever thinks that I'd like a day off," she said.

"Day off. Day off. Day off," said Jed, flapping his wings busily, sending a few feathers flying. He cocked his head on one side, stared at Grandma and then began to sing tunelessly. He sometimes sang in Liam's voice and sometimes in an odd voice that no one recognised. He insisted singing the whole song and his weird rusty voice irritated everyone.

"Gin a body meet a body . . ."

Grandma Bridie picked up the bird's nighttime cover and put it over the cage. There was instant silence.

"I can't take that today," she said, rather irritably.

"He'll sulk," Bran said. "He'll be noisier than ever when you take it off."

"I'm sulking," Grandma said. "It's a lovely day and I want to walk in the country, not make Cornish pasties for people who don't even say thank you. People who come in and expect me to drop everything and make coffee. People who never put their clothes away and bring home football shorts covered in mud."

Bran stared at her. This didn't sound like Grandma at all. She slapped the ball of pastry down on the board as if it disgusted her.

He buttered a second piece of toast.

"I need all the table, young man," Grandma said. " So get moving. There's an army to cook for here. And wash up your plate and cup before you go, please."

Go where? Bran wondered, cramming the last piece of toast into his mouth. He washed his plate and cup and saucer and put them on the draining board. Grandma handed him the tea towel, and looked at him with one eyebrow raised. She was definitely not in a good mood today.

He put the dishes carefully in the cupboard and closed the door very quietly in case Grandma thought he had slammed it on purpose. He looked at her. Her back was rigid, and the rolling pin thumped down on the pastry, over and over again.

Jed uttered a dispirited squawk. He hoped someone would take pity on him and let him see the world again.

Bran had hoped for so much this Saturday. He should have realised nobody would be at home. No one ever asked where he was going. No one ever asked him to go anywhere.

He hated games and he hated football. He enjoyed going out with his father, visiting the farms, but that didn't happen often. He wanted a dog of his own. He wanted to work with animals. He wanted to play with animals. Not with the cats; they soon tired of their games and walked off, leaving him on his own again.

None of the boys in his class interested him. They only seemed to like computer games and football and watching television. None of them even had a guinea pig, let alone a dog. He felt like an alien from Mars.

He much preferred being with the animals, and longed for the day when he could be a real vet and help his father.

A dog would be just his, and it would be company.

He thought about the House of Secrets, the spacious grounds, the space all around it, the large paddock where he could play with his dog.

Outside a car hooted and brakes squealed. Then he heard the constant drone of traffic coming up the hill, the gears changing, the engines sometimes groaning. Down the road, the drums began to beat again, an insistent throbbing that made his head ache.

"It takes time to recover," his mother's voice said, inside his head. "You were very ill, and that cold you had was much more than just a cold. Be patient."

He hated being tired. He hated being patient. He hated everybody and everything and today he even hated Grandma Bridie. Nobody listened to him. Nobody wanted to hear about their new home. His father had forgotten about it, or maybe had just been humouring him, a silly little boy with a silly dream.

Perhaps he could help in the little hospital. Meg let him prepare the food for the animals, and when they began to feel better, he talked to them and cuddled the little ones. He loved that, especially the kittens that came in for neutering. They were always lonely because they belonged to people who petted and fussed over them, and cages were strange, unfriendly places.

He walked into the waiting room, and saw one of his greatest friends, a police dog-handler, with a lovely German Shepherd bitch who was obviously soon to have puppies. Sam Gredy had been retired for two years. He now owned a training and boarding kennels for dogs just a mile away from the House of Secrets.

"I didn't know you had any bitches." Bran stroked the soft fur on her head. "Is she yours?"

The German Shepherd lowered her ears, so that they lay flat against her head, and she licked his hands. She obviously adored being stroked. Bran was careful not to pat her on the head or shoulders. Dogs hated that. He tickled her chest and she leant against him. He thought longingly about his imaginary Troy.

"I struck lucky," Sam said. "This is Dina. Her owner asked me to care for her before she died. She'd mated her to Conn. It was such a shame. She was a lovely old lady and was really looking forward to this litter. She had a stroke three weeks ago but didn't recover." He sighed. "She was nearly ninety and had had a good life. I wish she'd lived those few weeks longer. She bred Conn as well. One of the best breeders I know . . . knew."

Bran loved Conn. He was Sam's clever competition dog, so wise that sometimes Bran felt he was cleverer than some humans. He certainly knew a great deal more when he was nosing out a trail, trying to find where someone had walked and hidden his favourite stuffed woolly rabbit. Conn had stolen it from one of Sam's grandchildren.

Sam offered him all kinds of more suitable toys, but Bunbun remained his true love. The little boy who had named his toy Bunbun was happy to give it up, and the silly name just stuck. Often Conn walked around the house with it in his mouth, a rather idiotic look on his face and his tail waving. He glanced out of the corner of his eyes at Sam, as though he knew his master felt the toy inappropriate.

"Thinks he's a gundog, daft animal," Sam often said, with laughter in his voice. Conn just wagged his tail and clamped his jaws more firmly round his rabbit. He loved catching it when someone threw it to him. It was much the worse for wear. Bran wondered what would happen when it finally came to pieces. So far Annie, Sam's wife, had always managed to repair it.

Bran looked at Dina wistfully. He wanted a dog more than he wanted anything on earth. A puppy to bring up as his own. A puppy like Conn.

"When are the puppies due?" he asked.

"In about ten days. I just want Maldwyn to check her over and make sure there are no signs of anything wrong, or if the pups might be coming earlier. It looks as though it will be a big litter."

"Can I come and play with them?"

"When they're a month old, yes, providing you do exactly as I tell you. Pups that children play with sometimes grow up to hate all children, because the children's games were too rough and the puppies got hurt. Dina needs to be left alone with them at first. They'll be blind for ten days and deaf for the first three weeks. Then they'll start to be more fun."

"We must move to the House of Secrets," Jed yelled. He was annoyed because Grandma Bridie was slapping pastry around and ignoring him. Jed's screeching voice could be heard all through the house.

"What did Jed say?" Sam looked astonished.

"Dad and I saw the House of Secrets the other day," Bran said. "He might buy it; I hope he will. It would be much better living there than here."

"It needs a lot doing to it. It's been empty for five years. But I'm told they're reducing the price, so it could be a bargain." He frowned. "Someone told me the owners might auction it. They want to get rid of it soon, as they work in Brussels now and are likely to be there for a long time. We'd be neighbours. It's only a few hundred yards away from me, if you cross the field by the lake and use the footpath."

"I didn't know it was so near," Bran said.

"I'm downhill and there's a copse of trees hiding us. You can't see my place from there, and you can't see the House of Secrets from our home."

"I don't expect we'll move." Bran sounded

disconsolate. "Dad was only letting me dream. He'll never find time to do all the work it needs, or even to sell this place and move. Nobody *ever* has time in this house."

Sam rumpled Bran's hair. He hated Grandma doing that, but Sam was different.

"Cheer up. You'll feel better soon and then everything will look different. Pneumonia isn't funny."

"Nobody said I had pneumonia!"

"They probably didn't want to scare you. Good job your mother's a doctor, or you would have been much worse. She knew what was wrong at the stage when most parents would still be deciding whether to call the doctor."

Bran looked across the room. His father came out of the operating theatre, holding the unconscious Burmese cat in his arms. There was a large shaved area on her side, criss-crossed by a row of tiny stitches. One leg was in plaster.

"Bran . . . you're not going anywhere?" Josh Murray's voice sounded anxious.

Bran shook his head.

"Can you keep an eye on puss for a while? Everyone's so busy this morning. Let Meg know when she starts to come round from the anaesthetic. And make sure she doesn't twitch or make any unusual noises. She's very badly shocked and I'm worried about her. She's also in kitten. I hope she doesn't lose them. She's a show cat."

"I'll get my book," Bran said. He liked sitting in the big chair in the little hospital room, and felt important when his father asked him to help. It would be useful to learn as much as he could before going to college.

"I told Sam about the House of Secrets," he said. "I got the details about it from the estate agent yesterday." He brought them out of his pocket.

"Good boy. I hadn't forgotten, but everything seems to have happened at once. I'll look at them at lunch. I've a call to make first. The bull at Inch Farm managed to tear his leg on some barbed wire. He tried to jump in the next field where someone who didn't know much about animals had herded two cows that strayed from another farm. Joe Makin says it'll need a good few stitches, and that bull's not exactly my favourite patient."

"Life's like that," Sam said, looking at the disappointment on Bran's face. "Think of the pups. Maybe if you do move you could have one. I'll help you train her."

"A dog?" Bran asked, knowing they were

talking about daydreams, but very willing to pretend.

"A bitch is easier. They're smaller and often more docile. Maybe she could have pups one day."

He'd still call her Troy. A real pup, all his own. It was a thought to cherish even though he knew it wouldn't happen.

Bran fetched his book and went into the little hospital room. The only other patient was a very thin, sad puppy that wagged his tail half-heartedly, not sure if he was doing wrong.

"Someone found him wandering down the road near their home," Josh said, as he came in to check the cat. "He lookes half starved. He's been running wild for some days. I suppose someone just chucked him out. There's a plate of food there; you can give him about two teaspoons every hour. It's going to take weeks to get him fit, poor little beast."

Bran was used to abandoned animals. They often came to his father for treatment before being taken back by rescue organisations, like the RSPCA. He put a hand through the mesh of the cage and the pup licked it, then retreated to the far wall, as if sure he would be harmed.

Meg ran in, stoked the Aga, put several

towels and some overalls in the washing machine and turned it on.

"No time to breathe. Make yourself useful, Bran, " she said. "Make coffee. Four of us. Surgery's just about over. You, Maldwyn, Helen and me. Grandma's in a cloud of flour and she's in a funny mood. I think we'd better not add to her chores today! She's muttering about slavery again."

The cat was moving its front paws. Bran looked at them, suddenly wondering if he knew what a twitch looked like? Should he call Meg back? Sometimes animals died after an anaesthetic. Sometimes even while they were under it. Not often, but it had happened.

He felt edgy and unhappy. Grandma seldom had moods but when she did they lasted several days. Then it felt as if there were black clouds over them all. Everyone went out and she stayed at home. She worked her fingers to the bone for all of them. She said so repeatedly when what she called the "black dog" took over. They were never grateful; she fed them, looked after them, cleaned and tidied after them. Time she went away and lived on her own in a nice little flat. She would be able to put her feet up and play bridge every afternoon and nobody would expect her to make tea or coffee or cakes, *or* anything else. They should learn to manage on their own.

Bran sighed.

He knew just how she felt, because he was usually the one she talked to most. He didn't seem to have any interests away from home, like the other children.

Meg's kettle had boiled. Bran spooned instant coffee into four mugs. Maldwyn liked his black and Helen liked sugar. Meg had saccharine as she was trying to lose weight, in spite of which she had brought in four doughnuts.

They finished at eleven o'clock. Meg brought in another cat and put it in a cage.

"He had an argument with a tractor. A farm cat. They're always in trouble," she said. "His leg's broken, so we'll have to X-ray and set it. He doesn't seem to be in great pain and he can't move around in there. Let's have coffee first."

They had just finished wiping up the coffee mugs when Grandma Bridie stormed in.

"And when are you all coming for coffee?" she demanded. "It's been sitting there for ten minutes with my newly-baked scones that I made for a treat and there's not a soul near me. Have I got the plague or something?"

She flounced out of the room and they all

looked at one another guiltily.

"Can't win," Meg said. "I wish I hadn't had two doughnuts!"

They trooped into the kitchen. Grandma Bridie buttered scones for all of them, adding jam and cream. Bran was sure he would not want another mouthful all day. There would be trouble at lunch-time when he tried to eat his Cornish pasty.

"I'm going shopping," Gran said. "No one's to touch the pasties or the cake. I'll be back in about an hour."

They waited until her little car drove out of the yard. Bran took the cover off the Mynah's cage and raced back to the hospital to look at the cat. She was still lying quietly, with no sign of trouble.

Maldwyn, who could eat five times more than any of them, buttered himself another scone.

"Greedy pigs," Jed said.

They laughed.

"You can say that again," said Meg.

Bran looked out of the window. He had returned to the room to report. A man was running across the yard, carrying a large dog in his arms, which lay as if lifeless. He raced into the waiting room, ringing the bell violently as he came in at the front door.

"He was pulling on his slip chain," the man said. "He stopped breathing. He saw a cat, and pulled me across the road. Luckily just outside . . ."

Maldwyn had the dog on the floor and was working on him. He breathed into his mouth. The ribs rose and fell and the dog gasped. A moment later he sat up, and stared at them all, bewildered.

"I think he has to learn some manners," Maldwyn said. "The chain cut off his breath. I've seen it before. Put a harness on him, or a Halti, and go off to dog class."

"Never a dull moment," shouted Jed.

Bran, back in the hospital, kept his eyes constantly on the cat, who appeared to be waking slowly. He hoped that the rest of the day would be very dull indeed. As Grandma Bridie often said, you can have too much of a good thing.

He took out the photographs of the House of Secrets and studied them.

"My secret," he thought. "The first secret. I wonder what others there will be?"

Or maybe there'd be none at all. Perhaps Romana could tell him how to wish and make wishes come true.

If only he could visit her.

CHAPTER 7

The House of Secrets. It dominated his thoughts and it figured in all his dreams. Why was no one interested? Why was no one trying to buy it? What was wrong with his family?

His father had promised to look at the brochure. But there had been one emergency after another, and he had ended up with no time at all.

The days seemed to pass so slowly.

Sunday had to be better, Bran told himself. On Sunday his mother would be home and his father was not on duty. Maldwyn was taking the only surgery they had, at twelve o'clock. Maybe they could all go and look at the house.

He knew the day was not going to be as he had planned when he heard the telephone ringing just before six in the morning.

He heard Grandma Bridie's voice.

"Time for a coffee?"

His father answered her, yawning. So they wanted the vet, not the doctor. At least his mother would be free.

"A quick one. That was Jock McKenzie from Trayhill Farm. He's had dogs in his flock; several sheep dead and a number injured."

Bran's bedroom door was open. He could hear the voices clearly.

"Did he catch the dogs?"

"No. There will be more injuries soon. Two strays, he thinks. Probably dumped by owners who got tired of them, poor devils. Not their fault. Today I don't like people."

Bran couldn't get back to sleep. He dressed, arriving downstairs just as his father's Land Rover drove out into the street. Grandma Bridie was hugging a mug of coffee as if her hands were cold.

"More in the pot, love," she said. "You heard?"

Bran nodded. At times he found both his parents' work unbearable. How could people be so careless with their animals? How could you just *throw* away a dog that had lived with you, leaving it to run wild? And his mother was always upset when one of her patients died, as if she were to blame: even when there was nothing any doctor could do, or when the invalid was very old.

"I thought I heard Mum go out, earlier," he said. "Or was I dreaming?"

"No. You weren't dreaming. There was an emergency call about four o'clock. I sometimes wonder if the rest of the world sleeps all night. Nobody ever seems to in this house."

She took the cover off the Mynah cage.

"We must move to the House of Dreams," Jed said.

"The House of Secrets," said Bran, correcting the bird.

"What is this House of Secrets?" Grandma Bridie asked.

Bran took the brochure out of the folder that he used for his school project. Everyone had to choose their own subject. He was busy writing about the history of the police dog. One day he would have his own German Shepherd.

Soon. When Dina's pups were born. When they moved to the House of Secrets. It might turn out to be the House of Dreams. Dreams that never came true. Jed's mistake worried him, but then the Mynah never did talk sense. Much of what he said just happened to fit in with what the humans around him said.

"What's everyone doing today?" Bran asked, feeling forlorn. His mother would sleep the morning away. A savaged flock meant hours of work, and his father would be tired and irritable when he came home. Josh hated unnecessary work and sheep worried by dogs were unnecessary. He cared passionately about the injured ewes, knowing they were terrified and suffering. In an ideal world everyone would look after their animals properly.

"Liam's away for the whole weekend. Tony's father rang up yesterday afternoon to say they had found a lovely little bed and breakfast place and asked if Liam could stay with them. Georgie has a nine mile ride for charity. All the stable horses are involved. Jenna's going out. I don't know where."

Bran wished he was as old as Jenna. He'd be able to help his father so much more. Maybe go out with him when he had to tidy up a savaged flock. Maybe be more use to him than he was now.

He hated being twelve. There was so much he couldn't do because he wasn't big enough, or old enough, or strong enough.

Grandma was looking at the photographs of the House of Secrets.

"Tell me about it," she said.

"It's lovely. There's lots of room in the house. Dad said the big barn would convert into a surgery and waiting room; there's room for a small hospital annexe." He sat remembering his face suddenly flushed with excitement. "There's a walled garden and room for dogs. The cats wouldn't have to be shut in a pen all the time. There's an orchard, and just beyond the garden there's a lake with swans."

"Suppose you and I go and have a look at it?" Grandma Bridie picked up her coffee mug and took it to the sink. "As soon as breakfast is over. There's pasties and sandwiches for lunch and no need for me to cook till this evening. I'd like to see this dream house of yours."

Her small face was rosy under her white hair, and her eyes bright; as she contemplated a whole day away from her chores. Grandma does everything for all of us, Bran thought, shocked to notice there were blue marks under her eyes. When the smile went and the flush died away, he saw that her face was pale and tired.

"House of Dreams. House of Dreams," Jed

sang. "Jed's lonely. Nobody loves Jed."

"You're a bore," Bran held out a piece of apple for him. He snatched it greedily. Jed's head was on one side, the apple sticking out of his mouth like a cigarette. "We'd all love you a lot more if you weren't so noisy."

He glanced through the window. The day had brightened up a bit. There was a hint of sun breaking through the morning mist. Bran took the cats their breakfast while Grandma Bridie packed a small bag with food.

"We'll play truant," she said. "It's *weeks* since I had a day off. I think it's going to be a fine day. We'll picnic by the lake and feed the swans. We've got too much stale bread."

Bran suddenly wanted everyone to leave the house. Jenna hardly spoke as she ate her breakfast, seeming to be in a dream world of her own. Georgie, flying down at the last minute, grabbed a slice of toast on her way out through the door.

At last they were ready. The little yellow Mini threaded through the traffic in the town and drove out into the country lanes. The sun had fulfilled its promise and shone from a clear sky.

They pulled up outside the gate. The notice board seemed to lean more than ever into the hedge. Grandma Bridie looked at the house.

"It needs work," she said. "But such possibilities."

She was out of the car, suddenly full of energy, her face bright with expectation.

"Someone loved this garden. There are all kinds of plants here, among the weeds. Look, a Christmas rose. Lenten lilies. Little alpines. Choked with weeds, poor things."

Her fingers itched to help them, to free them from the all-embracing chickweed and bindweed, from thistle and nettle, that hid them from the sun.

Bran followed her down the crazy-paving path, and watched her as she peered in at windows and ran her fingers over the plaque that read House of Secrets. Then she walked to the boundary fence, looked out at the fields, the lake, blue under the sky and the swans swimming serenely on its surface.

"You like it?" a voice asked behind them and Bran spun round to face Romana, laughing at them, her hair braided with ribbons the same colour as the scarlet of her patchwork jacket.

"I like it." Grandma Bridie was laughing too. "Do you come with the house?"

"Romana lives in the woods. She caretakes, sort of," Bran said. "How's your hare?"

"He died, poor little fellow. He had been hurt inside, and I didn't know. I took him to your father's partner. He said nobody could have done anything for him. So we gave him his peace. He was in too much pain. He's free now."

Grandma Bridie glanced at her watch.

"Twelve o'clock already. Lunch. Everyone should be home for our evening meal and I haven't made anything ready yet, so we'll have to go back early."

"I was going to eat here too," Romana said. "I love the lake and the swans and they know me. The cob isn't very friendly when his mate has babies, but he's quiet enough now."

Grandma Bridie had brought pasties and egg sandwiches. Romana had made a flan which she cut into three, sharing it among them. There were little rock cakes, light as a kitten's breath, and gingerbread fingers and short-bread. There were peaches and bananas.

Grandma always packed enough food for an army even when there were only two of them.

"Dad will never have time to buy the house." Bran's voice recognised that they were all just dreaming. Jed's accidental name was right. "He's always busy. Always something, like today." A cloud passed over the sun, darkening the sky. Life is like that, Bran thought. Nothing wonderful ever lasted.

"Maybe he could make me his agent," Grandma Bridie said. "We never did use the money that I got when I sold my own house. Your dad told me to keep it for a rainy day. I think there'd be enough to make sure we can own this. It's perfect. Maybe Jed was right and House of Dreams suits it better."

"I like House of Secrets," Bran said. "Dreams are never real. Secrets can be."

"Wisdom out of the mouths of babes," Romana said, her dark eyes glinting as she looked at Grandma. A message seemed to pass between them that Bran didn't understand. He knew suddenly that they would be friends, even if they never came to live in the house.

"You can't re-name it. That would be unlucky." Romana held a roll in her hand and stretched out her arm. The two swans left the water and waddled over to them, ungainly on land and far bigger than Bran had realised. Gently, one of them took the bread in its beak. Romana held out a second roll. The long white neck stretched out and the other bird accepted its trophy. There were more clouds across the sun. The sky was darkening, promising rain.

Behind them, the House of Secrets seemed to fill with shadows.

"Sun and shade. Light and dark," Romana said. "Life's a patchwork and nobody can have happiness all the time. You only know you're happy when you've been sad as well. Just as you can't know how wonderful it is to be well unless you've known what it feels like to be very ill."

Grandma Bridie picked a daisy and held it up.

"I could live here. With flowers, and maybe kittens. I've always wanted to breed Burmese cats. There's the garden to bring back to life; the orchard to treasure, the walled garden where we could grow our own fruit and vegetables."

"I thought you'd like to grow orchids," Bran said. "You always wanted to."

"I want to grow kittens more," Grandma said. "Kittens are fun and alive and playful. Orchids are beautiful, but they are cold flowers. I think I prefer marigolds."

Romana picked the daisies, making them into a chain. She wove a crown and put on her dark hair and laughed at them.

"Queen of the May," Grandma Bridie said.

Romana took off the daisy crown and put it on Grandma Bridie's head.

"It suits you."

"I feel like a very old and rather silly fairy," Grandma said, laughing, as she removed the flowers. She hung them on a willow tree.

"I'll leave them there as a wish, a hope. Maybe a promise."

"A fairy godmother," Bran said. "Waving a wand and making the House of Secrets ours. Georgie could have her horse, and Jenna whatever she wants. Maybe a studio to paint in. Liam has so much space to explore, and to be safe in. You can have your Burmese brood queen."

"And you?" Grandma asked, her eyes on Bran as if she were looking right into his mind.

He thought of Dina and her pups growing inside her, soon to be born. He thought of a pup of his own, of playing with him, of training him. The small bubble of excitement in him grew.

He smiled up at his grandmother and then at Romana.

"That," he said, "is a secret."

CHAPTER 8

Romana collected the remains of her picnic and packed it neatly in a wicker basket. Bran was sure she had made it herself. He watched her as she walked away towards the wood, then she turned and waved to them.

He walked behind Grandma Bridie, carrying her basket for her. He was looking at the house and the gardens, not at the ground. He didn't see the bramble that snaked along the ground, gripped his ankle and threw him down. He landed on his side, all the breath knocked out of him. The lawn was edged with large boulders that had once been painted white. He had fallen against one of these.

His arm hurt and he felt sick. He sat up, aware of Grandma's worried face, but feeling too much pain to reassure her. He was faintly surprised to see Romana running along the path towards him.

"I picked up your picnic plates by mistake," she said. "I came to return them. Just as well."

She put her arm round Bran and helped him to stand up.

"My arm hurts," he said.

"We'll go to my caravan. I've something there that will help. I don't think it's broken, but you did fall very heavily. Your side and arm will be badly bruised."

Bran wondered if he would be able to go to school in the morning – if he would ever go back to school. Something always seemed to happen to prevent him going back every time. They walked slowly, so that he could stop and rest.

The sun had disappeared and a thin rain was falling. He was cold. The trees at the edge of the wood were dark and forbidding, telling him he wasn't welcome. Nothing seemed quite real.

They walked along a soft path, deep in dead leaves. Then suddenly the trees parted, and there was Romana's caravan, bright with new paint, sitting in a glade.

"I had a horse once, but when he died, I decided to stay, " she said.

A brown lurcher came to greet her, his rough coat long and shaggy. He put his wise head against her hands, and then came to nose Bran, sniffing every inch of him. He seemed able to tell who Bran was and where he had been.

"Lie down, Merlin," Romana said and the dog sighed and eased his long body to the ground.

"He guards me," Romana said, opening the door with a long thin key that had a hawk's head instead of a handle.

She helped Bran up the steps and then held out a hand to Grandma Bridie, who was panting behind them. Bran realised they had been walking uphill. The house lay below them. The lake was dull now under a grey sky and patterned with drops where the rain had fallen.

"I'll make tea," the gypsy woman said. "But first, let's look at those bruises."

She filled the kettle and lit the gas. Bran was fascinated by the inside of the caravan. Everything was so small, so neat, so compact. The bunk was covered in patchwork and spread with a bright quilt. It was scattered with cushions embroidered with birds and butterflies which looked as if they might take wing into the room.

Romana's hands were gentle. She soaked a white cloth in an odd-smelling liquid and bandaged it against his side. She bandaged another on to his arm. It was cool and soothing.

"What is it?" Grandma Bridie asked.

"Arnica lotion. It's wonderful for bruises. And these are wonderful for shock," she added, dropping two tiny pills into a spoon and handing it to Bran. "Put them on your tongue and let them dissolve. You'll soon feel better. Nothing's broken."

She poured water into the teapot and produced white mugs patterned with poppies. She added several drops from a tiny phial to Bran's tea.

"My grandmother's magic potion. They call it 'Rescue Remedy'," she said. "It works miracles with very sick animals and it's good for people too. It won't hurt you. Nothing I ever use can hurt anyone."

The pain eased. Merlin put his shaggy head over the half-door of the caravan, his eyes pleading. He was rewarded with a large bone, which he took to the edge of the clearing and lay down to gnaw.

"There's a back road to the caravan," Romana said. "I'll show your Gran, and we can bring the car almost to the door here. Rest. We won't be long. Merlin will take care of you."

She whistled and the dog bounded up to the door. She opened it and Merlin lay down under the table, out of the way.

"Look after Bran," she said.

The long tail thumped noisily against the floor. Bran felt remote, as if nothing around him was quite real. Maybe the caravan was a magic place and he was in another world. The dog came to him and put his head on Bran's knee. The fur was rough, nothing like the fur on Dina's smooth head.

The arnica pads felt cold but the pain was going. He could move his arm and no longer felt sick. He felt as if he had been here before, and knew every inch of the caravan: the tiny carved animals that sat on the shelves, the seal and the otter, the dolphin and the bear, the deer and the bull that stood with his head lowered, as if about to charge.

"Time to go," his grandmother said, startling him. It seemed only a moment ago since she and Romana left and he had not heard the car arrive.

"He fell asleep." Romana smiled at him. "It's the quickest way to get well."

He felt dreamy on the way home, his mind full of the House of Secrets and the plans he was making for it. He didn't answer his grand-mother when she spoke and she felt sure Romana was wrong: Gran thought he *was* badly hurt.

His mother was home. She removed the arnica pads to examine him carefully.

"An old-fashioned remedy I'd forgotten about," she said, and then replaced them. "You'll have some pretty colours tomorrow on your side and your arm, but there's nothing much wrong there. Your gypsy friend seems to know what she's doing."

"Jed's lonely. Poor Jed," said the Mynah, determined to be part of the family again. No-body had been taking any notice of him, even though he had wolf-whistled and miaowed and clucked like a chicken to get their attention.

"Jed's daft," Bran's mother said, and stroked the bird with her finger. He put his head on one side and began to recite in Liam's voice:

"Five for silver, six for gold,
Seven for a secret never to be told."

Bran turned his head to look at Jed, who was perched with his head on one side. He flapped his wings, scattering feathers.

"Secret. Secret. Secret. House of Secrets." His raucous voice echoed through the kitchen, mocking them.

CHAPTER 9

Bran's side and arm ached. The bruises were dark purple and yellow.

"Spectacular," Grandma Bridie said, sponging him down with arnica. "Spectacular" became Jed's new word.

Bran thought about the House of Secrets whenever he had time. Did Grandma mean what she said? Would she speak to his parents? They both seemed busier than ever. It was lambing time and his father was out at all hours. The little outhouse seemed to have a permanent visitor in there, some ewe that was in trouble. Bran knew that the ewes changed from day to day, but the place was never empty. Their bleats sounded odd in the town street.

"In the old days the vet went to the farm," Grandma said, as yet another lamb came in for treatment. "Nobody has time now. The mountain has to come to Mohammed."

Bran stared at her, wondering what on earth she meant.

There was both a flu epidemic and a mumps epidemic so his mother was busy too. Bran was rather glad he'd already had mumps.

Grandma Bridie was tired. She moved slowly, and snapped at them all.

"Those drums go on for ever," she said angrily on the Friday evening, slapping down a plate of shepherd's pie in front of Bran, who was the only one home. Liam had gone to spend the evening with his friend Tony. Jenna was never there these days and Georgie had a dressage lesson in the indoor riding school.

She walked out of the room, leaving Bran alone.

"It's a lovely idea," said Jed, in Bran's father's voice. "We can't let you do it, Bridie."

He squawked and flapped his wings, then changed to Grandma's voice.

"I can't stand the noise here any more."

Bran thought that Grandma had come back

into the room, but it was Jed again.

Bran finished his meal and washed up his plate.

Then Grandma Bridie came back.

"Don't say a word," she said. "The group has been practising all day and my nerves feel as if someone has been picking them into tiny pieces. If anything else goes wrong today, I'll scream."

"We can't afford to move to the House of Secrets," Jed said in Josh Murray's voice.

"That bird could cause a divorce," Grandma Bridie said.

"They don't want to move?" Bran asked.

"It's not something we can decide in an instant," she said. "It needs a great deal of alteration if your father is to carry on his practice there. The house needs a new roof, and some of the window-frames are rotten. It's been empty for five years and it's damp."

"Damp, damp, damp," yelled Jed.

Grandma put the cover over him.

"If we *did* move there we'd need two big caravans, not just one. There are too many of us for one. The barn has to be converted into a surgery and waiting room, and the little hospital would have to be built for the animals recovering from anaesthetic."

That was one of his father's dreams. At the moment, recovering animals were in cages in the office, in the little kitchen where they washed the bedding and the overalls, and where they prepared food for any animals that had to stay in. There were even, occasionally, animals recovering in the downstairs bathroom. Cages were in any corner that would hold them. Even a neutered tomcat needed time to recover before he could go home.

"We need planning permission. We might not get it." Grandma was busy with the next meal, walking from cupboard to table with flour and lard and eggs.

"So it's impossible," Bran said, seeing his dreams shattered.

"I didn't say that. I said it needs a lot of thought. I want to buy it, and maybe move over there into a caravan and supervise the alterations, while your father and mother work from here. That's what they won't allow. They won't take my money."

"It would be your house," Bran said.

"Only until this one was sold. But who would buy it? We don't want another vet setting up here, as we'll still be very close, and I don't think the town is big enough for two practices."

Bran glanced at the clock.

"I thought surgery was over."

He had heard the doorbell ring.

"Sam rang. He's bringing Dina in. It's an emergency."

Bran rushed out of the room into the waiting room as Sam came in with Dina. Her eyes were glazed and staring. She had a bone in her mouth. As Bran looked at her, she lay down and began to savage it as if she wanted to tear it to shreds. Her legs were twitching. She looked as if she were out of her mind.

Josh was already in the waiting room, a syringe in his hand. He knelt down and injected the contents into the bitch. She ignored him, intent on her bone.

Bran stood watching, terrified. This wasn't the Dina he knew. He was afraid she was going to die, or maybe lose all her puppies. Neither Josh nor Sam saw him. Both were watching the bitch. She appeared quite mad.

Suddenly she stopped gnawing the bone and looked at it as if she had never seen it before. The glare died out of her eyes. The twitching stopped. She stood, and walked over to Bran, then put her nose in his hand.

"What was wrong?" he asked. "Will she be all right?"

"She'll be fine now," his father said. "She

had eclampsia. That's lack of calcium in brood bitches. Other female animals can get it as well. Sam knew what was wrong and got here fast. The injection works like magic."

"I was lucky," Sam said. "I've been out all day, and she didn't show any signs until the middle of my tea. If she'd started this morning, or in the middle of the night . . ."

"What would have happened?" Bran asked. It was the first time he had seen an animal affected.

"She'd have lapsed into unconsciousness and then into a coma. In the old days they died of it. But we know what to do now, and providing we see the patient very early, we can save her and her babies." Josh was stroking the bitch. "We'll have some wonderful pups from you, won't we, old girl?"

"She seemed to know what she needed. The first thing she did was to round up every bone in the place and attack them as if she were demented. I've never seen anything like it." Sam patted Dina gently. "Gave me a real scare, you did, old lass."

"We'll inject her regularly," Josh said. "A number of the farmers here give their cows calcium as a routine just after calving. It saves a lot of trouble."

He glanced at the clock, and then at Sam.

"Come and have a coffee. I'd like to keep an eye on her for an hour or so."

"We must buy the House of Secrets," said Jed, in Bran's voice. Both men looked at Bran, but he was drinking and the voice went on.

"Peace. No more noise. No more drums. Peace. Please, God." That was Grandma Bridie's voice. She sounded desperate. Jed picked up each person's mood when he repeated their sentences.

Startled, the two men looked at one another and Grandma poured coffee into two more mugs. Her face was rather pink.

"That bird . . . I'm sure he knows what he's doing. He's a born troublemaker."

"It would be a good place to live," Sam said. "If we move I can have a puppy," Bran said.

"Look, son," Josh said, his voice patient. "We have to have the house surveyed if we are even going to think about it. It might not be worth having. It could have dry rot, or wet rot, or be in such a poor state that we'd need a fortune to put it right."

The telephone rang and Bran answered it. He listened for what seemed like a very long time.

"I'll tell him at once," he said.

"Trouble?" Josh asked.

"It's Georgie. Someone opened the gate of the top paddock. A lad on a motorbike. The horses got out and the boy's friends herded them, riding their bikes behind them so that the horses all bolted down the road. One of the ponies jumped a barbed-wire fence, and she landed upside down in mud. She hasn't had a lesson. They've been rounding them up. The one that's badly hurt is Lindsay, who Georgie usually rides. She's shivering and shocked, and she has some bad gashes on her hind legs."

Josh was already out of the room, gathering up his equipment.

"Dina's OK," he said. "Don't worry about her, Sam. Any recurrence and get straight over here. That injection should last her at least a couple of weeks."

He was halfway through the door as he spoke.

"Dad, can I come?"

"If you're quick."

Grandma handed him his anorak. He gave her a quick grin and ran.

His father had already started the Land Rover. Bran jumped in and fastened his seat belt.

"Georgie loves that horse as if it were her own," he said.

"I know."

"She was going to jump her at the Agricultural Show. She's been practising that, and dressage." Although Bran had no desire to ride, he loved horses as much as his twin, and enjoyed being with them.

They turned in at the gate of the riding stables and Josh jumped out. Bran followed him, careful not to make any sudden noise that might alarm the already badly-frightened animals.

The lights were on in the special stable kept for sick or injured horses. Georgie and Lois, who ran the stables, were both covered in mud. There on the straw, head hanging, was quite the sorriest and dirtiest horse that Bran had ever seen. Blood from two enormous gashes seeped on to the floor.

Bran knew, from his father's expression, that this was far worse than he had imagined. Georgie stood beside the horse, stroking her neck.

"We've been trying to get the mud off her for hours. She's plastered," Lois said.

"Will she be OK, Dad?" Georgie asked.

"I can't promise," he said. "She's exhausted, she's shocked and those cuts are going to cause problems for weeks to come. It depends how deep they are and how strong she is."

"Will she be fit for the Show?"

"Ten weeks away? Or is it only nine? I very much doubt it. She's going to need rest and careful handling, to make sure she isn't over-stretched. Also, what is this fright going to do to her behaviour? She may never trust the world again."

Georgie walked out of the stable, hiding tears. Lois looked after her, wanting to comfort her, but there was work to do. Bran stood by the horse's head as his father injected her. Josh set up the anaesthetic apparatus, and Lois helped him.

Lindsay lost consciousness. Bran helped tie her legs to four posts, and watched as his father began to clean the gashes and stitch them up.

"I hope she can stand the treatment. But I've no choice," Josh said.

"I've lost one of the others," Lois said, her voice trembling. "My beautiful hunter. He broke his leg. They had to shoot him."

She and looked at Bran.

"Life's not fair," she said. "Why pick on a

prank like that? The police won't catch them. Nobody knows who they are. They had helmets on. No one got their numbers. The man who saw them herding the horses rang the police at once. As soon as they heard the sirens, they were away. He said they were laughing . . . Laughing! I could kill them."

"Was he insured?" Josh asked.

"Yes, but that's not the point. I'd have won with him at the Show this year. I've worked and worked on him . . . all those hours . . . wasted."

Lois followed Georgie into the darkness outside.

"Life's never fair, son," Josh said, aware of Bran's distress. He looked down at the horse, now stretched out in the straw.

"Can I stay and help clean her up?" Georgie asked, coming back into the stable. "Lois says I can have a bed here. I can borrow night things."

"Sure, stay," her father said and gave her a hug. "Ring in the morning and let me know how she is."

"One minute the whole world is ready to give you what you want and the next it takes it away again," Josh said as they drove back to their home.

Bran thought of Dina. So much could go wrong before the pups were born. Even afterwards things go wrong. Some litters never thrived, but died one by one, within a few days of birth and nobody knew why.

Even if she had her pups, he couldn't have one. They weren't going to move to the House of Secrets. None of *his* dreams would ever come true, either.

CHAPTER 10

The drums throbbed until after midnight. Bran heard the police drive up, and the angry voices. If only they could move. Sometimes the noise was worse after the police had gone, as the boys provoked their neighbours. Bran fell asleep at last and dreamt of the House of Secrets.

He woke very early to hear the telephone shrilling a summons to one of his parents again. Liam was staying with Tony again. Bran switched on his light.

Five o'clock. Why did people and animals have to be ill at such awkward times? He dragged on his dressing gown, yawning and rubbing eyes that felt stiff with sleep. He went downstairs, hoping to be there before Grandma, so that *he* could make coffee for whichever parent had been called out. Then he could tell Gran to go back to bed and get some rest.

"It's Lois," his father said. "Lindsay's gone into deep shock. She's afraid she'll die."

Bran poured boiling water on to the coffee powder, added milk and two spoonfuls of sugar.

"Can I come?"

"If you can dress before I drink this."

Bran raced upstairs. No time to wash. His grandmother put an untidy head out of her bedroom door.

"Need me?"

"No. I made Dad's coffee. It's OK."

"Thanks, Bran. I could do with a rest." She smiled at him and closed the door again.

He dragged a comb through his hair, pulled on his clothes and was downstairs again before his father was halfway through his drink.

They went out as quietly as they could, careful not to slam doors. The sleeping street was silent, which seemed strange to Bran. He had never been out at this time before. No lights in the curtained windows, no cars or lorries. Just one post van, ahead of them, and a man in a raincoat, due on an early shift, yawning at the bus stop.

Down the street, where the newsagent was already busy sorting out the daily paper round. Turn the corner, and past the church with its poster outside giving the times of services.

Bran felt early-morning stupid and wished he had been able to sleep the night before. He yawned, and his father caught the yawn. They both laughed.

The lights flashed green and the Land Rover surged forward on to the brief stretch of motorway that would bring them to the stables. The day had already begun on the motorway and there was far more traffic, most of it heavy-duty vehicles. The Land Rover overtook a tanker, and they settled to a steady seventy miles an hour.

They took the next slip road, and within minutes they were in a different world, their headlights shining on trees and hedges. Beyond them the light reflected from the eyes of animals watching them pass.

The farms were already busy, lights on in their yards, cattle moving towards the milking parlours. It's another world, Bran thought. The town had been almost dead, with hardly anyone about. The country was well awake. Once they had to stop while cattle were herded back to the field, milking having already finished.

The stables were bright with lights. Lois met them as they turned in at the big gate, which was propped open ready for them. Bran knew it was closed at night, and as Lois had had trouble with intruders, it was padlocked. That did not keep people out, but it did prevent horses being stolen.

All the horses had been brought in the night before. In summer they usually stayed out in the fields. It meant more work and Lois worked alone. It also meant stables to clean and food to be brought for each horse, as well as buckets of water. The chores were endless.

"She hasn't stopped shivering," Lois said. "We got her dry and we've rugged her and I've put the heating on. Luckily she isn't plunging around. She's almost too quiet and she won't eat or drink."

Georgie was sitting on a straw bale, stroking Lindsay's neck. She wore one of Lois's bulky anoraks over her own clothes. Blood had seeped through the bandages on the horse's hind legs.

"She's going to die," she said, her voice desperate.

"Not if I can help it," Josh said.

Bran had never seen a more miserable looking animal. Her head hung low, her eyes were dull and she took no notice of them at all when they came into the stable. The floor was thick with straw.

The horse did not even move when the needle went in.

"I hope that will do the trick," Josh said. He looked at his daughter. "You have any sleep last night?"

"We took it in turns to sit with her," Lois said. "But I'm not sure that either of us slept even when we did go to bed."

"Breakfast for everyone," a voice said. Bran looked away from Lindsay to see Romana, unfamiliar in breeches and shirt, but wearing her man's tweed jacket. The elbows were patched with leather and it was too big for her. She wore a cap on her head, her hair pushed underneath it. Her bright eyes glittered at them.

"Go and eat, all of you." she said. "I'll sit with her. Maybe she'll take some of my grand-mother's corpse reviver. It won't hurt her, I promise," she added, looking at Josh. She wasn't sure how a qualified vet would feel about country remedies.

"If you can get her interested in living I'll be grateful," Josh said.

"I don't want to eat," Georgie said.

"I made it for all of you. Eat," said Romana. "Maybe you could do with some of Lindsay's special brew too."

"Romana comes and goes like a miracle." Lois led the way across the yard towards the house. "She only turns up when we need her badly. I don't know how she does it."

She's a guardian angel, and she looks after the House of Secrets as well, Bran thought, as they walked into the bright kitchen. Romana had prepared the fire, cooked bacon and eggs, potato cakes and tomatoes. The plates were keeping hot on top of the stove. The smell made him suddenly very hungry indeed, and even Georgie looked happier.

The table was already laid for them, with coffee powder in the mugs, waiting for water to be added.

Lois's whippet bitch lay in her bed, watching them. She never moved unless strangers were about. Then she turned into a barking demon, anxious to drive the intruders away. A big tabby cat sat in the armchair, purring and kneading the cushion he lay on.

He jumped down, walked towards Lois and wrapped himself round her legs. She picked up a bowl from the draining board and filled it with cat food. This prompted the whippet to race over and paw at her leg.

"I haven't forgotten you," she said. "Even if it is far earlier than your usual feeding time."

"There's nothing more we can do," said Josh. "I've given Lindsay a hefty dose of antibiotic. She's had her tetanus protection regularly and she's a strong animal. She has had a terrible time. How long was she in the mud?"

"It took about four hours to free her; it was like quicksand. We don't know how long she'd been there before Pat McIntyre found her when she was cycling to work. She's the shepherd at Linney's."

Bran knew the Linney farm. They had more sheep than anyone else around. Pedigree swaledales. They often won prizes at the county fairs. Mark Linney was in his form at school and was always bragging about them. Which was hard on Dan Palin, also in the same form, whose father had a small struggling farm and sheep that never won anything. Mules, Mark said with scorn, using the official name for cross-breds. For all that they were healthy sheep and yielded good wool, Bran's father said.

The whippet sat beside Bran hoping for some food to drop on the floor. He could see her brown eyes watching every forkful as it went from plate to mouth.

"Don't feed her," Lois said. "She's a glutton, and I don't like dogs that beg at the table." She sighed. "I've had to cancel all my lessons. There isn't a horse fit to ride after their mad gallop. Can you look at them all, please Josh, and make sure there aren't any hidden injuries?"

"Were they all let out?" Josh asked.

"Every last one of my working horses. Luckily the little rescued mare that I bought last week was in a stable behind the house, and not in one of the paddocks. She's already suffered from humans. I don't know *what* she'd have done if she'd been with the others. I doubt if I'd be able to cure her of her fears, though now there is a chance. It was quite deliberate. They were in three separate paddocks. Every gate was opened. The people who heard them said it sounded like a rodeo, as they galloped along the road. How do you round up a mob of terrified horses, hellbent on racing away from you?"

"How did they?"

"Several of the local farmers joined in; they brought dogs and opened all the gates of empty fields. Then Bryony, who was leading them, saw grass and headed for a field and they all followed her. I had horseboxes delivering them all day yesterday. Heaven knows what it will cost."

"How many?" Josh asked.

"Eight without Magpie. My lovely hunter. I wish I were a witch. I'd put a death spell on all of them. They don't deserve to live. I'll have to send him to the knacker's yard. I'm hoping Magpie's insurance will cover the bills."

She stacked the plates angrily.

"It won't make up for losing him. Nothing will." She slammed the door as she went out of the kitchen.

"Dad, will Lindsay be lame?" Georgie asked.

"I hope not. I don't think so, but nothing's ever certain. I won't pretend because I don't know for sure."

He looked at his daughter's expression.

"Life's tough, Georgie, and it's unpredictable. You don't want me to pretend everything's all right when it might not be, do you? I think that would be much more cruel."

Georgie sighed.

"I'd rather know. Lindsay's been my horse ever since I started here. She's special. I'd hate not to be able to ride her."

"Come and look at her," Romana said,

appearing in the kitchen doorway. "I won't promise anything, but I think she's perking up."

Lois, who was filling a bucket with water, put it down and followed them. Lindsay was standing tugging steadily at her haynet. She turned her head to look at them, and then went on eating, pulling gently at the wisps, not very interested, but at least making some effort.

"My magic or yours?" Josh asked Romana, smiling at her. "Maybe a bit of both. Plus Georgie and Lois's efforts. And her own strong body. She's a tough little horse." She stroked the soft neck.

The sound of the telephone shrilling in the yard startled all of them. Lois ran to the tack room to answer it.

"It's for you," she said, handing the phone to Josh. He listened, his face serious.

"I'll leave at once." He replaced the receiver and looked at the concerned faces.

"It's Dina. She's started to whelp but the third pup's too big and has jammed. We'll have to do a Caesarian. I hope Meg's at home. I need her. It would happen on a Saturday."

"I'll ring Meg," Lois said. "You get off."

The day seemed to be made up of speedy

journeys, fighting time. Fighting bad luck. Fighting nature.

Bran willed the Land Rover to go faster. Hurry, hurry, hurry, said a voice inside his head. Or Dina might die and there would be no puppies at all.

Why did nothing ever go right?

CHAPTER 11

Sam was waiting for them when they reached home. His face was anxious. Dina, with two pups, lay in a big box in the back of his estate car. He and Josh carried the box into the surgery, neither of them saying a word. Meg drove up as Bran removed his father's case from the Land Rover, which he then locked.

"Meg, I want you for the anaesthetic. Sam, take those two pups into the recovery room, and put the box by the Aga. Bran, find another box, fill three rubber hot-water bottles and cover them well with blankets. It's a case of all hands on deck."

Bran ran into the kitchen. There were usually

some grocery boxes at the back of the little utility room beyond it. He was just lifting one out when he was startled by a voice.

"I'm going out, Jed. I don't care what they say, any of them. I'll do it my way and I don't care if you tell them so."

It was Grandma's voice, her tone defiant. What on earth was she talking about?

"I can cope here," Sam said, as Bran went back to him. "Not much I can do except make sure the pups are kept warm. Your Dad'll need that box."

Bran wanted to go into the surgery but he wasn't wearing sterile clothes. Meg appeared suddenly with three puppies in her arms. She gave them to Sam and took the box from Bran, who had already filled the rubber bottles and wrapped them well in an old blanket. The soft puppy blanket was on top.

"It's a big litter. Can you clean these up? Make sure they're breathing."

"Gin a body . . ." Jed croaked out in the horrible voice they all hated. He flapped his wings, suddenly and inexplicably excited, and mimicked a dog barking, a phone ringing and a motorbike racing its engine, all within a few short seconds.

"Oh, shut up," Bran said wearily. Trust Jed

to put on one of his worst performances when everyone was busy. Maybe he did it to get some attention.

For once he could show Sam what to do. He had helped his father before. He took a tissue and rubbed it gently over the tiny squirming body, cleaning away the transparent membrane that wrapped it. Bran had scrubbed his hands carefully and he inserted a finger in the puppy's open mouth.

"You have to clean the mucus away," he said. The pups felt slimy. Sam took the next pup and began to clean it up. "Hold it upside down, so that it drains out of its mouth."

The pup Bran was holding sneezed. The tiny body was so small that he was afraid of damaging it as he passed the tissue lightly over the wet fur.

"That's great. He's breathing now."

The small mouth was already searching around, looking for milk. The head looked odd with its blind eyes and squashed ears, quite unlike a German Shepherd. The pup grabbed Bran's finger and began to suck.

"Jed's alone. Nobody loves him. Poor Jed." The Mynah was frantic, sounding as though he were in the room with them, rather than in the kitchen.

"Come on," Meg said, handing Bran four more pups. We've just got to stitch her up."

"I hope she'll be all right," Sam said, busily cleaning the four tiny animals that now lay in a second box. "I couldn't bear to lose her." The earliest pups were now squeaking, desperate for food.

"You clean them," Bran said. "I'd better make up some bottles in case Dina can't feed them."

The milk powder was always kept ready. Bran mixed the feed and sterilised the tiny bottles. The teats were always tricky to put on.

"Good boy," his father said, as he carried Dina into the hospital. She lay so still that Bran had a frightening moment when he was sure she was dead. "We won't need the milk you've made up. Put it in the fridge, ready for later."

"She's fine," Josh added, seeing Sam's anxious face. He examined his work carefully. The long slit in her stomach was now only visible as a mass of minute cross stitches, holding the two sides of the wound together. "See what a lovely tidy job I've made of it!"

Bran smiled to himself. His father was justifiably proud of his surgery and rightly so, but his mother was always teasing her husband about his arrogance.

The boxes were put by Dina's head under the lamp that was used to warm patients as they were coming round from anaesthetic.

"They'll do fine for a while," Meg said. "As soon as she's properly awake we'll introduce them to her and let them feed. They're going to be a lot of work for Sam. He won't be able to let them stay with her all the time until that wound has begun to heal. It doesn't affect the milk supply, luckily, and I think she has plenty of that. We took some off her while she was unconscious. We can use that to feed the pups."

Bran knew that the first milk contained a substance called colostrum that helped the puppies to fend off illnesses. He looked down at them. Nine of them. Meg filled the bottles. They could feed four pups at a time. He wanted to feed the odd one himself, so that he had three, not two, to look after.

One of these could be his. Which one? He was fascinated by all of them, by their tiny paws and the transparent claws, by the eager heads and the small squeals.

"Very much alive and kicking," Josh said in a satisfied voice. "Just wait four weeks. They'll be all over the place."

Bran lifted the first pup that he had cleaned.

This was a little bitch. She swung her small head and clenched her lips on the teat and began to suck vigorously. Maybe this one was Troy. He wasn't yet sure. Perhaps it would be better to wait a few days before deciding.

The pup was already his. He was making plans, even though he knew he might be disappointed.

Meg was having more trouble with her puppy, one of the smaller dogs. He seemed unable to hold on tight and kept dropping the teat.

Josh was holding the biggest.

"This is the fellow that caused all the trouble. Well and truly jammed. He's a whopper. Four bitches and five dogs. Most of them weigh about a pound and a quarter but this one was well over two pounds. He's a massive fellow."

Bran could think of nothing but the pups, all fed and back in the boxes under the lamp. They were a huddled mass of black and gold, their eyes tightly closed, muttering and murmuring and wriggling against one another, trying to burrow deeper into the living pile.

"I wish Dina's owner could see them," Sam said, looking down at them proudly as though he were the father and not Conn. "I miss her."

Josh was making coffee.

"She was a great old lady. I miss her too. One of my nicest clients. She always thanked me for anything extra, and gave me a bottle of her home-made wine if she called me out in the night or over a holiday." He sighed. "Ah well, none of us lives for ever. Luckily it's Dina's second litter and she's a good mother. We might've had problems if it had been her first. As it is, I think she'll just get on with her job without a fuss, and enjoy them."

When they had finished their coffee they went back into the hospital room.

Josh put his hand against Dina's head.

"I remember the night she was born. A wicked night. I drove through torrential rain and hail. Her mother started to whelp and then stopped completely. She needed an injection to have Dina, who was the last and the smallest of the pups. You wouldn't think so now."

Josh seemed fascinated by the biggest pup. He grinned at Sam.

"I've named him for you. Titan. He has the makings of a truly enormous dog. He could never have come out normally, so we did the right thing. He seems very much alive. Going to be a troublemaker when he grows up, I'd guess."

Sam took Dina and her pups home that

evening. Bran had taken several looks at them, though he did not go in to the hospital room again once Dina woke up. Meg was sitting with her, and she let each pup suck in turn several times. Dina could not yet cuddle them. They might hurt her stomach. She licked each one, and when they were put back in their boxes she lay watching them, now and then putting her head in to nose them, just to make sure they were all hers and all well.

Sam had said nothing at all about Bran's pup. Had he forgotten? The next three weeks seemed odd. There was change in the air, but Bran couldn't quite make out where the feeling came from. Grandma Bridie had very little to say and almost snapped when anyone spoke to her. She did everything at top speed and spent far more time than usual out of the house. There was always food for them, but her work was done at odd times, rather than according to her normal routine. She had a secret, but what it was he couldn't guess.

Lindsay was much better, but was not yet fit to ride. There was no sign of lameness. Georgie had taken over her care and walked her daily, both before and after school. Just short gentle walks to get her back into work again one day. The gashes had healed, leaving angry scars.

Each day seemed endless.

Term was over at last. Bran passed all his exams, if not with flying colours, at least with better results than anyone had expected. He came down on the third morning of his holidays to see Sam's estate car in the yard. He ran into the waiting room.

Sam sat by the window, Conn beside him. The big dog greeted Bran with enthusiastically.

"I thought something might be wrong with Dina."

It was four weeks since that eventful day, but it seemed much longer.

"She's fine and so are the pups. When are you coming to choose yours?"

"Did you mean it? How can I have one here?"

"I've been thinking about that. I owe your dad for a lot of things. How about you and me as partners in the puppy? He or she can live with me. You can come and see it as much as you like. Then maybe one day he or she can come and live with you, when the puppy stage is over."

"Can we keep it a secret?" Bran asked, sure that if he told his family everyone would at once say no.

"Why not?" Sam had been first in the waiting

room. Now another owner came in, with a big Rhodesian Ridgeback that made a face at Conn, lifting one lip and growling softly. His owner scolded him and the dog settled down, his eyes on Conn, who ignored him.

"Is Conn ill?"

"No. It's just time for his booster. I never let that lapse. Too many nasty things around for them to catch. Get your Grandma to bring you to the kennels tomorrow. Come for the day. I'm off duty. You can help me walk some of the dogs. I've got several small ones in that would be easy to manage. A nice little Westie, a charming little Cocker Spaniel and an Australian Terrier."

"What does that look like?"

"This one's a bit like a brown Cairn: short legs, terrier head, wiry coat that it's impossible to get to lie sleek and smooth. Game little fellow, and great fun. He's called Digger."

It would be good to work at the kennels over the holiday. Perhaps he could go every day. Bran was often bored and he liked to be busy.

"Tomorrow," Sam said when he was leaving. Bran was waiting by his car in the yard. He wanted to ask Sam to take him home with him immediately, but then there would have been problems getting back home.

He went back into the kitchen. Jed eyed him, his head on one side again.

"I'm worried about Bran. He doesn't seem interested in anything," the bird said in Josh Murray's voice.

"Give him time." It was now Grandma speaking. "He hasn't found out what it is he wants yet."

Oh yes I have, thought Bran. None of you has ever *asked* me what it is I want. He thought of Dina, and the need for one of her pups was so desperate that it hurt.

Grandma Bridie was out again. If only she would come home. Then he could ask her if she'd mind taking him over to Sam's. He worried all afternoon. Suppose she said no?

CHAPTER 12

Bran woke with a feeling of excitement. Grandma had said yes, but to be up early, and early meant very early indeed. Six o'clock. Sam started his kennel work then, so it wouldn't matter if Bran was there before most people's days began.

The kitchen was already warm and full of the smell of baking cakes and scones. Grandma Bridie grinned at him.

"When you get old you forget how to sleep," she said. "I prefer to get up and do something useful instead of just lying there." She opened the oven door and slipped a clean knife into the cake that was cooking on the lower shelf. It came out faintly smeared. "A few minutes more. Glad you decided not to keep me waiting," she said. "Big breakfast?"

Bran shook his head. He was too excited to eat. He was dying to tell his grandmother about the puppy, but it had to be a secret. Maybe even *she* would say no.

He cut two slices of bread and put them in the toaster. Grandma took several trays out of the big family oven and put scones, rock cakes and little flans to cool on a wire tray. She bolted the catflap so none of the cats could come in and steal them.

The toaster popped up suddenly, shooting both slices into the air. Bran, who had forgotten his toast, jumped.

"More, more, more," shouted Jed. The toaster incident had triggered one of his wing-flapping manias.

"Gin a body . . ." he croaked, and then changed his mind and sang "Three Blind Mice" in Tony's voice. Liam's friend had been to tea several days before.

Grandma laughed.

"Tony spent an hour singing that in the hope Jed would learn it, but the wretched bird wouldn't say a word all evening. Poor Tony was really disappointed. We'll have to tell him Jed did learn it after all."

"Bet he'll never say it when Tony's here," Bran said, chewing hard. His whole body was bubbling inside. His own puppy. It was like having all his birthdays and Christmases rolled into one. He did manage to eat both slices of toast which Grandma had smothered in butter and marmalade, but with difficulty. If he didn't eat she'd think he was ill again and would probably send him back to bed, or take his temperature. That, he was positive, must be sky-high.

The fluttery feeling inside him grew and grew. He longed to race round the room, to shout at Grandma to hurry up, to drag her out to the car. When at last they *were* ready he was sure the engine wouldn't start, or they'd run out of petrol. He was too busy with his own thoughts to wonder where Grandma went on her jaunts.

"You're early, young man," said Sam, as Bran raced down the sloping drive that dipped towards the farmhouse, forgetting to wave as Grandma drove off.

Sam lived in an old converted farmhouse set in the middle of several small paddocks, which were used both to graze sheep and exercise dogs. Oliver, the retired police horse, grazed in the field nearest to the house. A shaggy-coated Shetland pony standing beside him was dwarfed.

"One of our friends rescued that little fellow," Sam said. "He was going to be sold for meat. Joe couldn't bear that and bought him. Silly thing is, Joe lives in the town and had nowhere to put him. So Oliver has a companion. He loves that little fellow. His name's Bracken."

"Why Oliver?" Bran asked. He always thought it a silly name for a horse.

"He was bought as a hunter before he came into the police. He was already called Oliver Cromwell. Don't ask me why. He's nearly twenty now; bit late to change. I'll be sad when he goes. He's a great old fellow."

Oliver, who was standing at the fence, suddenly nodded his head, exactly as if he were agreeing.

"I've lessons to give this morning," Sam said. There was a big training school on one side of the house and beyond it was the kennel block with room for thirty dogs. Alice, Sam's wife, came to the dustbin and smiled at Bran. Sam dwarfed his wife. His dark hair was grey at the ends, but Alice was still as blonde as she must have been as a child, Bran thought.

"I hear we three share a secret," she said. "Come and see the pups. They're gorgeous now and so funny."

The pups were in a big kennel, the floor of which was liberally spread with newspaper. Dina lay in a huge box, with three of them feeding from her. The other six were romping round the floor, tumbling over one another, pouncing and falling over, pulling at ears and tails.

"I'm keeping your father's name, Titan, for the big lad," Sam said. "He's booked. I'm going to keep him and train him for Schutzhund."

Bran knew that that was the German form of police-type training. The dog had to be very good indeed to gain a title. He wondered if he could train his puppy up for that.

"Something you might do in about ten years time," Sam continued, unaware he had just destroyed an ambition. The puppy would be too old for Schutzhund by then.

"There are lots of things you can train him for," he added, and Bran's hopes rose again. Something he could do that his twin sister couldn't. This pup would be the best-trained dog anyone had ever had.

"Take your time," Sam said. "No use choosing in a hurry. They all look good, but they'll be quite different characters when they grow up."

Small teeth pulled suddenly at Sam's shoe-lace. One of the little dogs was quite determined to get his shoe off.

"That's not for you," Sam said. "He comes after Titan in the pack. Nearly as much of a troublemaker, and if Dina didn't keep them in order, I think those two would fight and mean it. Titan wants all the toys and Blackie is determined to get them off him. If Titan drops something, little Blackie pounces on it and carries it off and tries to hide it, but Titan always finds it. It's a running battle to see who wins. So far, it's always Titan. He's much stronger."

Bran looked around the floor. There was a small piece of knotted rope lying by the dog bed. He picked it up, and one of the little bitches looked at him curiously and then came to nose it. She sat looking at him, as if expecting something to happen.

He threw it. She trotted after it. The others were all busy tugging at a large sock that Titan held firmly in his teeth. Sam watched as the pup picked up the rope and came back to him and pushed it into his hand. Her whole attitude said, "Come on, play with me. Throw it again."

Bran looked down at her, and she looked up at him, her head on one side. The pups did not look like German Shepherds yet. It would be some time before those flop ears came erect. Some never did. He didn't want a soft-eared dog. How could you tell at this age? He didn't like to ask Sam in case it was a silly question.

She was so tiny. Her head only just reached his ankle. He bent down to pick her up. Holding her gently, he was careful to make sure her small tail-end was cupped in his hand and that her back legs didn't dangle.

Sam held out a tiny yellow collar.

"Put it on her, if you're sure," he said. "Bring her over to the house. Alice is making coffee."

Bran had always intended to have a dog, not a bitch, but this little one seemed to have chosen him as her own. She snuggled against him, soft and warm, her fur smelling of clean puppy, a scent that no one could ever mistake.

"What are you going to call her?" Alice asked, producing shortbread and chocolate biscuits. Bran's queasy feeling had gone. He was extremely hungry. All the silly sayings came back to him. He felt nine miles high. Everything he had ever wanted was here, in his arms.

Her small warm tongue licking his nose and her bright eyes watching him as if trying to work out what kind of person was holding her.

There was only one name he could give her. His imaginary Troy had vanished forever, but here was the *real* Troy, the pup he had been waiting for. His daydream had been good preparation.

"Troy," said Sam thoughtfully. "Worth her weight in gold? It's a good name. It's easy to say, doesn't sound like any training command. Call a pup Kim and it sounds like 'come' if you aren't careful. Conn isn't the brightest of names. I use the Welsh 'tyd' when I want him. Then he can't confuse 'come' with 'Conn'."

Bran fed his pup, watching her clear the bowl fast. She trotted across the floor and discovered the food belonging to Sam's two cats. She emptied that bowl too, before they could prevent her.

He was going to hate going home again, but he could take the memory home to cherish, could dream of a real puppy, could see her every day throughout the holidays.

"I'm going to help Sam," he had told his father the night before. "I can walk the little dogs and wash the dog bowls. Holidays are boring. Everyone's busy except me."

"Wonderful idea," Josh had said heartily, glad his elder son had found an interest. Grandma had looked at him thoughtfully, as if she half-guessed. He had no intention of telling *anyone* that he was now half-owner of a puppy.

He put Troy back with the other pups, as she was tired, and helped Sam with the feeding bowls. There seemed to be endless chores. He walked one of the little Cocker Spaniels, and the day passed so fast that he couldn't believe it was time to go home again.

Grandma Bridie was waiting in the kitchen with Alice when Bran went indoors to fetch water for the dogs.

"Time to go," she said. "Quick, now, or we'll be late and everyone will be shouting for food. I haven't even begun to prepare the evening meal. You'll have to help me."

Grandma's face was flushed. She looked almost as excited as Bran felt. He saw her glance at Alice, and wink, and wondered what confidences they had been exchanging. He wanted to say goodbye to Troy.

"I'll take the water," Alice said. "Your grandma's in a hurry."

"Look sharp, young man. I've already waited twenty minutes for you." Grandma Bridie led the way to her little car so quickly that there wasn't even time for one last look at his puppy. But Bran treasured the thought of her all the way home.

CHAPTER 13

No one knew where Grandma Bridie went after dropping Bran at the kennels. Meg *did* wonder, as she had to make coffee for everyone and Grandma was never there. The only clue was a remark that Jed made, almost at the end of the school holidays.

"I'm getting old, Jed," the Mynah said in Grandma's voice. "Time to think of me for a change."

Only Bran heard it and he worried. How would they manage if Grandma Bridie left them? Would his parents find time to do the housework? To shop? To do all the many errands? Maybe they should help her more, but she always insisted that she preferred to manage alone. The others got in the way and often left part of the work unfinished so that she had to go over it again.

Guilt needled him, so that he became more thoughtful. He started suggesting Grandma sat down, that he made her a cup of tea, that she rested. She was puzzled by his attitude, unaware that Jed had betrayed her.

"Get away with you, boy," she said. "I'm not decrepit yet." Bran decided that maybe she had just had an off day and that nothing would change after all.

The House of Secrets had become an impossible dream and would never be theirs. His father had been appalled at all the estimates that came in for work to be done, and he refused to discuss the subject any more.

"We'll just have to go on looking," he said. "Something will come up that we can afford. That house is out of the question."

In spite of his disappointment Bran was enjoying himself immensely. Most of the time was able to forget his dream house. He and Georgie had been promised bicycles for their next birthday but until then Grandma or his mother or father dropped him off at the kennels. He wondered where Grandma was going, but she refused to tell him.

"If you don't ask questions, you won't be told lies," she said.

Liam, who loved making up stories, decided Grandma had taken up spying and was on secret missions. This made all of them giggle, even Jenna, at the thought of Grandma listening into conversations and saving the country from some terrible fate.

Grandma made sure they were all busy. Jenna was helping at the Great Dane Kennels, Georgie at the stables, where Lindsay was now almost recovered, and Liam, to nobody's surprise, spent most of his days with Roy Marsh who had a pig farm. Liam, for reasons no one else could fathom, had a passion for pigs of all breeds, and knew more about them than many adults.

Bran loved the kennel work. He was with dogs for most of the time, and was able to walk the little ones. He watched Sam training Conn. Four times a day he was able to play with Troy, to take her into the big training school and roll balls for her, let her tug at her rope and watch her trot round, examining everything with her nose.

The school was so large and she was so small, but she had no fears. She was fascinated by the big bags of dog food that were stored in one corner, and was delighted when she found a box containing dog chews, one packet already opened. She stole herself a chew, eyeing Bran, puffing out one cheek as she did so and hid herself behind the dog-food sacks to eat in peace.

She raced happily round the room, content to follow him, or to run after him.

"Never chase her," Sam said. "Always make sure she chases you, otherwise you'll teach her to run away and she won't come when you call her."

His favourite game was to let her move away from him as far as possible and then crouch down and call her excitedly, holding out a tiny piece of food.

"Troy, Troy, come," he called, and the puppy turned and looked at him, saw the food and raced as fast as her small legs could carry her. Boy and pup ended up in a delighted huddle of legs and arms, as Bran encircled her, stroking her and praising her, telling her she was a lovely puppy and so good to come when he wanted her.

She tired quickly and after about twenty minutes play, curled up into a ball to sleep, or lay on her back with her legs extended. She slept with her mouth half open, totally relaxed.

Bran wished that he didn't have to go back to school. He would only be able to see her at weekends once school started.

On the last day of the holidays Sam gave him a soft, light lead, and told him to fasten it to her collar.

"Just follow her," he told Bran. "Don't tug or try to make her go where you want yet. She isn't used to it and it could frighten her if you pull on her neck."

The puppy had never explored the yard. She saw the milk bottles waiting to be collected. Bran followed her over to them. She sniffed them, decided they were not at all interesting, and began to follow the trail of a dog that had just been taken for a walk by Liz, one of the kennel girls.

Troy was so intent on the scent that she did not notice they had reached the field where the horse and pony were kept. Oliver came to the fence, put his big head over it and sniffed at Troy.

She had never seen him so close before. He was enormous, his head so much bigger than she was. She panicked, dancing on her lead, squealing and trying to back away.

Bran lifted her and sat on the doorstep, twenty yards from the field, while Oliver huffed in disappointment and walked away from the fence. He loved dogs, especially puppies, and he also loved sheep and lambs.

The pup cuddled up against Bran, her small heart racing. She whimpered briefly, and then began to calm down. She watched Oliver, who had returned to the fence and was looking at her. His ears flickered to and fro, and he whinnied, very softly.

The pup put her head on one side.

Oliver whinnied again, and Troy's head tilted to the opposite side. She was fascinated. She climbed down from Bran's knees and began to walk back towards the horse. Oliver did not move.

As she reached the fence, Oliver put his head over again and huffed at her, very gently. She looked at him for a moment and then her small tongue licked his nose.

"Good," said Sam, who had come up unseen behind Bran and Troy and was watching them. "She had the sense to be afraid at first, but then to think it over and see that Oliver meant her no harm. A pup that's never afraid of anything is very dangerous. They run into danger all the time."

"Coffee time," Alice called from the kitchen doorway.

Coffee time was Troy's feeding time. Bran prepared the bowl and set it on the floor, watching her as she ate. She had a little walk immediately afterwards, as pups always emptied themselves as soon as they had fed. Bran brought her back, feeling proud of himself. He already knew her routine, and Sam trusted him to care for her whenever he was at the kennels.

Alice cut him a slice of ginger parkin.

"I'm delivering dog-food this morning, to the pet shop in Markton," Sam said. " Want to come and bring Troy? It'll introduce her to the car . . . or at least, my van. I'll take you out in the car next weekend. That's a different kind of movement. I doubt if she'll be car sick. None of Conn's pups ever has been."

Troy loved exploring new places. She investigated the van very thoroughly, the more so since it was filled with sacks of food. She settled at last in the space by Bran's feet. Sam had put a small box there and lined it with her blanket. She recognised that this place was hers.

"Can we go past the House of Secrets?" Bran asked.

"Why not? It's only a couple of miles out of our way."

Bran looked down at his pup. So much seemed to have happened since they first found the house. Even though Josh said they couldn't buy the place, Bran was dismayed when he saw that the board had been taken down. The gate had been re-hung and painted, and the front garden tidied. There was a workman's van at the door, with ladders and trestles piled beside it.

Bran couldn't believe it.

"It's sold," he said.

The disappointment made him feel sick.

CHAPTER 14

There was nobody about at all. Bran climbed out of Sam's van, wanting a last look at the house. New people would change everything. It wouldn't be his dream home any more. Sam came to stand beside him.

"I wonder who's bought it," he said. "I've not heard even a rumour."

Bran walked along the newly-cut hedge to look at the house once more. On the other side of the van, hidden from view as they drove up, was Grandma Bridie's yellow Mini. He stared at it, and a second later Grandma Bridie herself came out of the house and walked towards the little car. She glanced up and saw Bran.

"Bran!"

He turned and walked towards the gate and opened it. Romana came out of the house smiling at him.

"I think your guilty secret is discovered," she said to Grandma as Sam joined Bran and stood looking at the two women. Troy, determined not to be forgotten, climbed out of the van and stood at Bran's feet. He picked her up, as she could easily get lost in the undergrowth.

"You'd better come in," Grandma said. "We're having coffee. I'd forgotten to take the cake in to the house."

She lifted a tin out of the car and led the way indoors. The hall was newly painted. So was the kitchen, which looked bright and welcoming, with a fire lit in the Aga and the door open. There were new modern fittings.

"What are you doing here?" Bran asked.

"Since it's perfect for us all and your parents wouldn't even consider letting me buy it, I bought it!" Grandma Bridie said. She grinned at him, her face mischievous. "I'm not a little girl to be told what I can and can't do. They can buy it from me if they wish, or come and live here with me and I'll own it. Or they can stay where they are and I'll live here on my own. I've had enough of the town. It will be theirs when I die, in any case, so what's the difference? It will get us all away from the din, and it's far more convenient." She laughed. "Or it *will* be, once all this is finished."

"How are you going to tell them? When are you going to tell them?" Bran asked, as he took a piece of chocolate cake from the plate on the draining board. There were several deck chairs for them to sit on plus a stool that Romana had painted, and given to the house as a present.

Bran looked at it, admiring the gaily coloured flowers on the bright red background.

The bare rooms echoed when he explored. There were only two more left to be decorated. Everywhere looked bright and new. The kitchen would be completely furnished once a table and chairs were added. Grandma's rocker would look well beside the Aga. The cats would love that. There was already a bright peg rug on the floor, which Bran guessed had been made by Romana.

"I hope Jed's going to tell them," Grandma said. "I've been teaching him to sing 'Grandma's got a secret. She's bought the House of Secrets. We're all going to move.' With any luck one of them will have heard it before we get home."

"Knowing Jed, it's the last thing he'll dream

of saying. He'll be spouting all kinds of news, but not that," Sam said, munching chocolate cake.

Bran couldn't believe it. He looked around him, hoping desperately that his parents wouldn't refuse to move. Suppose they did? What then? He'd come and live with Grandma. But that would pose problems too.

"How did you do it so quickly?" he asked.

"The solicitor who sold it to the previous owners is an old friend of mine. He had all the paperwork, so he didn't need to find out about the house. That had been done a few years ago, and he had all the details. It was only a matter of signing the contract. That was ready too, as someone else was going to buy it but decided against it at the last minute."

"I've been decorating and now the painters have come in to do the difficult parts," Romana said. "Your Grandma came to see me, and we shared the secret. We'll be neighbours. Won't that be fun?"

"We're getting it ready to live in when we move. No need for caravans. The men have just begun on the barns. I'll have to tell your father now, as he needs to be involved in planning the surgery, offices and waiting rooms. Luckily the builders desperately needed the work, so there's no problem there. They're keen to get it done fast."

"It must be costing a fortune," Sam said, looking around him.

"I invested the money from my own house and I've been living rent-free for ten years now," Grandma said. "I knew we'd need somewhere else to live and I've been saving every penny from my pension towards it. My husband had a big life insurance. Josh and Sally wouldn't take anything towards my keep. They said I earned that. It's surprising how much you can save. Then there's the interest on the investments."

"I'd better be off," Sam said. " Or it will be too late for that delivery. Do you want to stay here, Bran? I'll take Troy back to the kennels."

"No boys under my feet," Grandma said. "I don't want anyone to share my secret yet. Be off with you," she laughed.

Bran was still bemused when she came to collect him.

"Would I be wrong in guessing you have a secret too?" she asked, as the Mini turned into the road that leading to the surgery. The drums were thundering, loud above the sound of the engine.

"I thought you looked proud holding that adorable bundle of mischief."

"Her name's Troy. I'm sharing her with Sam till I get somewhere I can have her for my own," Bran said. The excitement brewing all day began to surface. Their move might be sooner than he thought. How soon? Before Christmas?

"Can I tell them? Please?" Bran asked as they went indoors.

"Perhaps," Grandma said. "But not till I say you can. It's been lovely having a secret life of my own that no one knew about. Except Romana."

There was a huge casserole in the oven, which Meg had put in ready for them to take out when Grandma came home. Everyone was sitting round the kitchen table, waiting. For once there was no one missing. Liam made aeroplane noises which Jed echoed. Bran was surprised to see that Maldwyn had joined the family. He was usually eager to go home as soon as evening surgery ended.

Georgie had her sketch pad in front of her and was drawing horses. Jenna was lost in a dream. His mother had a pad in front of her and was making notes in her quick decisive handwriting. His father was pouring coffee into mugs.

"It's Maldwyn's birthday. We couldn't let him go home and eat alone," Josh said, handing a small parcel across the table. "From all of us."

Maldwyn took the brightly-coloured paper off carefully, then spread it out and folded it. Inside was a pair of binoculars.

"They're wonderful. Mine aren't all that good," he said, delighted. He always spent any spare time he had in the woods, looking for rare birds, and he kept a diary where he listed all the birds he saw.

"Grandma's got a secret. She's bought the House of Secrets. We're all going to move," sang Jed. He screeched and began again.

"Jed's lonely. No one loves him."

Everyone was staring at Grandma Bridie.

"Is that true?" Josh asked.

"Quite true. You can live with me for a change. I don't see any point in you buying it when you get it on my death anyway. I'm having enormous fun owning a house again. I was going to offer it to you when it was ready, but I don't want to wait."

They were all staring at her, speechless.

"Trust you, mother, to offer us paradise on a plate then leave us all unable to know how to thank you," Bran's mother said. There was laughter in her voice, and Josh was beginning to look as if he had just won the pools. He walked over to Grandma and hugged and kissed her.

"If we don't have rent to pay, we will pay for someone to help you with all the housework," he said. "I won't take no for an answer. You can do the cooking. Nobody else could do it as well as you."

"The surgeries and waiting room and offices are your department," Grandma said to Bran's father. "An architect has drawn up plans for you to look at. The house will be ready to live in soon and you can travel back here to start with. No need for this house to go on the market till we're finished with the work there and settled in."

"I don't think that's a problem," Josh said. "In fact, it solves one. Maldwyn's lost his little flat. It's the top floor of a big house and his landlady is selling up. Besides, I've not given Maldwyn all of his birthday present yet."

He took a large square parcel from the dresser. Maldwyn looked at it curiously, and then once again took off the paper neatly and spread it out and folded it up. Bran wondered how he could be so patient. He would have just screwed the paper up, anxious to find out what was inside.

Maldwyn stared at the board that lay in front of him.

The bright gold letters read:

Joshua K. Murray MRCVS
Maldwyn D. Evans MRCVS
Veterinary Surgeons

Josh had never put his assistants' names on the board because very few stayed more than a year or two. There was just a little plaque on the wall which could easily be changed to give the name of the person working for him at the time.

"You *did* say you'd like to stay on and become a partner one day," Josh said. "I hope I didn't mishear you. If we move you can live here, and rent it out. There's much more space here than in your little flat. We can run two surgeries. Later on maybe we can both have assistants and build up the practice. The farming work has been growing, and it's becoming a bit of a headache."

Maldwyn looked astounded. Then he grinned, a huge grin that spread over his face and looked as if it would never come off.

Only Jenna looked unhappy.

"No one asked me what I want," she said. "Suppose I'd rather stay here?"

"Don't you want to move?" her mother asked.

"I haven't seen the place."

"It's wonderful," Bran said, suddenly desperate to convince everyone that it was perfect. "Georgie can have a horse. There's a stable and a paddock. Liam can have whatever he wants. There's lots of room for dogs. Jenna can have a brood bitch and breed her." When he saw Jenna's face he knew he had guessed right. "There are studies for both Dad and Mum. I can have my puppy home . . ."

He hadn't meant to let that secret out.

"Puppy. Puppy. Puppy," shouted Jed. "We've got to move to the House of Secrets."

"What puppy?"

Bran told them. Suddenly they were all full of plans. Grandma dished out the casserole and everyone talked at once. When they moved . . .

"I brought this," said Romana's voice from the doorway. No one had heard her knocking. "Grandma left it by the sink. I was afraid it would get lost. "She handed Grandma her ruby ring.

"Come and join the fun," Josh said. "I suppose you've known all along?"

"I knew before it happened," Romana said. "It was written in the stars. The House of Secrets is coming to life again. It began with Grandma's Secret. And then there was Bran's secret. Who knows what other secrets lie in store in days to come?"

"Secrets. Secrets. Secrets," Jed said rapidly. He flapped his wings. "Poor Jed. He hasn't got a secret."

The laughter drowned his angry squawk.

Homecoming by Cynthia Voigt
£3.50

Dicey made her announcement to James, Sammy and Maybeth: "We're going to have to walk all the way to Bridgeport." But they had no money and the whole world was arranged for people who had money – or rather, for adults who had money. The world was arranged against kids. Well, she could handle it. She'd have to. Somehow.

Dicey's Song by Cynthia Voigt
£3.50

Still troubled about her mother, and anxious about the three younger children, Dicey seems to have no time for growing up – until an incident at school shows her what to do.

A Solitary Blue by Cynthia Voigt
£3.50

Jeff has always been a loner, ever since his mother walked out, leaving him with his taciturn and distant father. Then his mother invites him to Charleston. For one glorious summer, Jeff is happy, before his dreams are shattered.

The Runner by Cynthia Voigt
£3.50

Bullet Tillerman has little interest in anyone or anything except running. But this is the 1960s, and with racial war at home and the Vietnam War abroad, Bullet's beliefs have to change, particularly when he's asked to coach a new black runner at the school.

Some Other War
Linda Newbery

Seventeen-year-old twins Jack and Alice have their lives mapped out. Jack is a stable lad at the Morlands' country house, and Alice is chambermaid to Madeleine Morland. Had it not been for the First World War, they might have stayed there all their lives. But the war changed many things, and brought Jack and Alice independence from the rigid social structure of the times.

Jack joins up with the first flush of enthusiasm, and is sent to the trenches. Alice continues at the Morlands', but as the casualties mount up and it becomes obvious the war will not be over by Christmas, she feels she must do something to help and begins working as a nurse.

Linda Newbery's novel accurately and sympathetically portrays life at the time of the Great War through the eyes of young people.

£3.99

The Indian in the Cupboard
by Lynne Reid Banks

When Omri is given a toy Indian and a small cupboard for his birthday, it seems natural to keep the Indian safely in the cupboard. And when, amazingly, the little man comes to life, Omri is thrilled at the thought of all the wonderful games they can play. It isn't long, though, before he realises that being responsible for another human being, no matter how small, is no laughing matter...

Return of the Indian by Lynne Reid Banks

Just over a year after Omri and his best friend, Patrick, have renounced the alarming power of bringing their model people to life, the boys find the temptation quite irresistible. But this time, the boys discover the added excitement of transporting themselves to a different place and time, with dangerous results.

The Secret of the Indian
by Lynne Reid Banks

After a terrible battle, many of Little Bull's warriors are wounded. Omri must get them medical help, but he must also protect the secret of the Indian. When Patrick goes back in time to the Wild West and falls into terrible danger, keeping the secret safe becomes even more difficult for Omri.

All at £3.99

Children of Winter
by Berlie Doherty £2.99

Catherine and her family are walking in the Derbyshire countryside when a sudden storm breaks out. They are forced to take shelter in an old barn. Somehow she remembers sheltering there before, from something far more dangerous than a storm.

Granny Was a Buffer Girl
by Berlie Doherty
(Winner of the 1987 Carnegie Medal)
£2.75

Before she sets off for a year's adventure in France, Jess wants to share all the family secrets – three generations of emotion, love and experience.

Spellhorn
by Berlie Doherty £2.99

Blind Laura has followed Spellhorn the unicorn to join the Wild Ones on their journey to their beloved Wilderness. But Laura has to return to her home, and to do so she must fight against Flight, her bitterest enemy, and cross the dreaded Sea of Snakes.

Order Form

To order direct from the publishers, just make a list of the titles you want and fill in the form below:

Name ....

Address ....

....

....

Send to: Dept 6, HarperCollins Publishers Ltd, Westerhill Road, Bishopbriggs, Glasgow G64 2QT.

Please enclose a cheque or postal order to the value of the cover price, plus:

UK & BFPO: Add £1.00 for the first book, and 25p per copy for each addition book ordered.

Overseas and Eire: Add £2.95 service charge. Books will be sent by surface mail but quotes for airmail despatch will be given on request.

A 24-hour telephone ordering service is avail-able to Visa and Access card holders: 041-772 2281